HIGHWAYS TO HELL

BRYAN SMITH

deadite press

deadite press

DEADITE PRESS
205 NE BRYANT
PORTLAND, OR 97211
www.DEADITEPRESS.com

AN ERASERHEAD PRESS COMPANY
www.ERASERHEADPRESS.com

ISBN: 1-936383-68-3

Printed in the USA.

CONTENTS

CONTENTS

ABOUT THE STORIES

What you have in your hands here is the first comprehensive collection of my short fiction. It may very well be the last such collection, or at least the last for a very long time. This is because I have only intermittently written short fiction in the years since I started writing professionally. When I was writing my novels for Dorchester Publishing (Boo! Hiss! Boycott!), I was also working a full-time job and it was all I could do to carve out enough free time to write those things. The few times I wrote short stories during those years was because someone willing to pay me to do so asked. Examples would include the stories that bookend this collection, “Living Dead Bitch” and “Hell Ain’t A Bad Place To Be.”

In the case of the former, my friend Kent Gowran had a short-lived website devoted to publishing fiction inspired by Troma films and other trash cinema favorites. He was willing to pay the going professional rate, so I was happy to come up with something for him. As a bonus, “Living Dead Bitch” was a genuinely fun story to write, so much so that it could have been much longer. That’s a potential complication I run into with virtually every short piece I attempt these days. They all want to be bigger and longer as I get into writing them, to become novellas or full-fledged novels. I guess it’s fair to say that over time the novel has become the form with which I am most comfortable. In some cases, I just say ‘fuck it’ and let it happen, as happened with a zombie story I started recently with the intent of including it as an original fiction piece in this collection. It's on its way to being a novel now and that feels right for that particular piece. With "Living Dead Bitch", I forced myself to rein in that tendency and finish it as a short story (though I reserve the right to revisit the material one day and turn it into something bigger).

As for "Hell Ain't A Bad Place To Be", that story was written at the request of the artist known as GAK for inclusion in the *Infernally Yours* Edward Lee tribute anthology. At more than 8,000 words, it's a longish story, maybe a couple thousand words shy of novelette length. I've been a devoted Edward Lee fan since his novel *Coven* was released in mass market paperback by Diamond in 1991, and so it was an honor to be invited to participate in the tribute project. I enjoyed getting to play around a bit in Edward Lee's world and I think the story reflects my enthusiasm for the project. Of course, the title is lifted from the AC/DC song of the same name. As a teenager, AC/DC was my favorite band. They were loud, snotty, obnoxious, and drunk…everything you want in a rock and roll band (or at least that was the case in the days before rock and roll got all pussified and politically correct on us). The title of this collection obviously is also derived from one of their songs. Now they're a bunch of fabulously rich old men who record and tour now and then when they feel like it, rather than sneering punks, but I still love them. So it was fun to insert original AC/DC singer Bon Scott in the story as a singer with a regular nightclub gig in hell.

Another story in the collection, "Pizza Face", is notable for being my first professional-level sale. In January 2003, it was accepted for inclusion in the perennially forthcoming Richard Laymon tribute anthology *In Laymon's Terms*. Amazingly, as of this writing, it's looking as if *In Laymon's Terms* is finally about to be published. Advance reader copies are circulating and contributors are being asked to supply updated mailing information. Nonetheless, the story's appearance in this collection will likely still beat *In Laymon's Terms* to the marketplace. I have mixed feelings about that. It belongs in this collection, no doubt. But the belated publication of the piece will be bittersweet. When the story was accepted in early '03, my father was still alive. By the time *In Laymon's Terms* is released (summer of 2011, most likely), he'll be eight years gone from this world.

"Pizza Face" was specifically written as a Richard Laymon-style story for obvious reasons. It features some of the late writer's best known trademarks, such as bloody violence, fascination with certain aspects of the female anatomy, and outlandish situations. I've been a Laymon fan since 1982, when I read his novel *The Woods Are Dark.* If you've read virtually any of my books, his lingering influence on my work should be clear.

Although "Pizza Face" technically counts as my first professional sale, due to the fact that Cemetery Dance will actually publish the thing soon, that distinction nearly went to another story in this collection. "Slugger" has never appeared anywhere in any form, either in print or online. However, in 1990 it was accepted by New Blood Magazine editor Chris Lacher at the then professional rate of three cents a word. For those too young to remember, Lacher had cultivated quite the bad boy reputation in the small press horror world. In a way, he was kind of the Brian Keene of his time. He didn't mince words and was known to offend people from time to time. Back then I was convinced he would be one of the genre's next "rock stars", in the vein of John Skipp or Craig Spector. So I was thrilled when New Blood accepted the story. It felt like a big deal and I believed I was finally making some real progress in my quest toward "making it" as a writer. True to my luck back then, however, New Blood never published another issue and the story, of course, did not appear. It is presented here exactly as it was written in 1990. I have not attempted to polish or update it. I'm sure "Slugger" could use some polish, but I'm not interested in reworking a story I wrote so long ago. It is presented here primarily for historical purposes, or perhaps even for a bit of closure. It is what it is. Maybe you'll enjoy it, maybe you won't—I'm just glad it's finally in print.

The story called “Rattlehead” is a story from the mid-90’s that appeared in a now-defunct webzine called Dream Forge. In gathering material for this collection, I came across the original manuscript for the tale and opted to include it. It’s not a bad story and, I think, deserves a place in print. It certainly shows some growth from the “Slugger” era, and I recall the online response being quite positive.

Several other stories in the collection date from 2001 and 2002, and are more polished by far than either “Rattlehead” or “Slugger”. Some of these stories appeared online at the Horrorfind website (when the fiction section was edited by Brian Keene), and others appeared in my 2003 chapbook *Under The Skin*, another Undaunted Press publication. I remain mostly pleased with most of these stories. They were written well after I’d emerged from my developmental period and display a surer hand than that wielded by the 25-year-old who penned “Slugger”. The stories I’m referring to here include “Remorse”, “Jarhead”, “Sustenance”, “Brain Worms Crave Soul Food”, “Truth”, and “Left For Dead (Moon Child Ascending)”.

Careful readers will note that a number of these earlier stories do not contain quite as much gore or over-the-top violence as the books for which I’ve become best known. A lot of that is related to being a young, unknown writer. I wanted to sell these stories, and back then I didn’t know how much of the really crazy stuff I had in my head I could use. After I sold that first mass market novel, my confidence soared and I became unafraid to let the more twisted side of imagination take me wherever it wanted. However, while some of the older stories may not be as wild or as fucked-up as what you’d find in *Depraved* or *The Killing Kind*, I think they are entertaining stories most of you will dig.

One of the more recent stories, “Killers on the Road”, was actually written as a bonus feature that appeared on the Dorchester website around the time *The Killing Kind* was released in paperback. It features characters from that novel, who bump into characters from my earlier novel, *The Freakshow*, with predictably bloody results. It’s a fun little story, and this marks its first print appearance.

So, that about wraps it up. At the rate I write short stories, the next collection will probably be another decade from now. That's if there ever is another one. And though novels have become my preferred form, I am grateful to Deadite Press and, in particular, to editor Jeff Burk, for making this possible. This book was Jeff's idea, and I might never have seriously entertained the notion of a collection otherwise.

So if you don't like the book, blame him (better Jeff than me).

If you do like it, buy the man a beer.

—*Bryan Smith*

LIVING DEAD BITCH

PART ONE: RIDING THE LONG BLACK SERPENT

The two-lane stretch of twisting rural blacktop looked distorted through the Chevelle's windshield, not quite real, like something half-remembered from a dream, a rippling dark ribbon the night sometimes seemed to just swallow whole. Or maybe not. But the notion prompted a more disturbing possibility. Maybe the road wasn't really a road at all. Maybe it was the long, unfurled concrete tongue of some great, unknowable beast, and the Chevelle was headed straight into its yawning, tunnel-sized mouth.

Or maybe, thought Rick Prather, *I'm just really, really, drunk.*

As he thought this, Rick's chin dropped toward his chest.

Out like a light.

For one second.

Two.

Three.

Four...

Rick's head jerked up as he came awake with a gasp. He pushed the heels of his hands into his eyes and gave them a quick, hard massage. Then he blinked them open again and saw a pretty array of dancing, swirling colors. He stared at them for a moment and decided he could also be experiencing some sort of delayed effect from the lysergic acid he'd taken the night before. Yeah. Goddamn. He sort of felt like he was in a trippy early 70's music video. Black Sabbath doing "Paranoid" on some forgotten TV show, the visuals all wavy and swirly.

He blinked his eyes again and let his head wobble to the left. "Dude, I'm sort of fucked up over here."

Danny Spillane didn't hear him say this. And it wasn't because the Chevelle's radio was blaring "The 19th Most Powerful Woman In Rock" by the Supersuckers. Nope, Danny was slumped over in his seat, temple pressed to the driver's side window, mouth hanging slack, drool rolling down his chin.

Rick stared at his friend for a long, uncomprehending moment.

At last, a troubling notion occurred to him, slipping through the substance-induced fog engulfing his brain like a silent and insidiously patient Jack the Ripper moving through early morning White Chapel mist.

Danny was sort of passed out.

Rick stared at him a while longer.

Yeah. Passed out like a motherfucker.

Rick's eyes went wide with alarm. "We're gonna crash!"

He seized his friend's shoulder and gave him a hard shaking. "Wake up!"

Danny groaned in his sleep, but remained insensible. He pushed at Rick feebly and said something that sounded like, "Lemme 'lone."

Rick dialed the radio's volume down and summoned a scream from the bottom of his lungs, invested it with enough desperate, gibbering horror to shame a convention of scream queens, and let that bitch loose. It went off like a bomb in the Chevelle's interior, a concussive, echoing explosion of sound that seemed to go on forever. The sound bounced and ricocheted in the closed space, sent razor-sharp shards of aural debris spinning through the air.

Danny woke up.

Looked at him.

Frowned.

And said, "Dude? What the fuck?"

Rick was beside himself with panic. He rocked in his seat and thrust a finger at the Chevelle's windshield. "Get your eyes on the fucking road, motherfucker! Can't you see we're gonna fucking crash!?"

Danny straightened in his seat with a maddening degree of care and deliberation. He leaned forward and squinted at the dark road, propping his elbows on the steering wheel. His face was expressionless for a long moment. Or maybe not quite expressionless. He looked confused. Then the corners of his mouth began to tilt upward.

He rested his forehead on the steering wheel and began to laugh.

A surge of molten rage rendered Rick almost fully sober for the space of maybe three or four seconds. "WHAT!? STOP LAUGHING, YOU DERANGED PYSCHO MOTHER-FUCKER!!"

Danny fell back against his seat, his body convulsing with laughter.

I'm gonna have to strangle him, Rick thought. *Take the wheel myself and save our sorry asses.*

Danny wiped tears from his eyes and managed to say two words between peels of maniacal laughter. "We're...stopped..."

Rick scowled at him. "What? No...that's..." Rick forced his gaze away from his delirious friend and peered through the windshield at the road. Huh. The view beyond the curved glass did evoke a certain...stillness. He cranked the window on his side down and stuck his head outside. He stared at the unmoving landscape of towering trees beyond the road's shoulder. It was a warm night. The soft breeze felt good on his flushed face. The terror-induced tension deserted him at once, and he again felt the mellow embrace of too much alcohol.

He settled back in his seat and stared straight ahead. "We're stopped."

"No shit."

They both started laughing then.

It went on for a while.

Rick slapped his thighs and coughed, choking on too much mirth.

Danny leaned over the steering wheel, squinted again. "We're sort of in the middle of the fucking road. Our lives have turned into a fucking Cheech and Chong movie."

Rick hiccuped. "Better that than fucking Scarface or...I

dunno...fucking Drugstore Cowboy. That'd be some grim motherfucking shit. Um...we should move."

"Yeah."

The laughter bubbled out of them again, went on for another indefinable period.

Then Rick said, "But seriously..."

"Yeah."

"We need a kickstart."

Danny was nodding by now. "Set us up."

Rick opened the Chevelle's glove box and sorted through the profusion of pill bottles and plastic baggies. Too many of them contained various strains of ganja, all of them super high quality, but not what they needed right now. He began to despair, thinking maybe they were out of what he was looking for. He began to panic again, but then he spied it, a nearly depleted baggie of white powder hiding beneath a much thicker, plastic-wrapped wad of green Indica bud. He snagged the bag of Bolivian Marching Powder from the glove box, fished a tiny spoon from the tray under the radio, and did a quick bump. He then passed the baggie to Danny, who did the same. They passed the baggie back and forth until the quantity of coke it contained had been severely reduced.

By then they were feeling much, much more alert.

Rick looked at his friend.

"Dude."

"Okay."

Danny started the car, put it in gear, and began to drive.

Rick was feeling a lot better now. He sat back, scrunched down in his seat a bit, and folded his hands over his early-stage potbelly. He stared at the dark road, deciding it no longer looked like the unfurled tongue of some great, unknowable beast. What kind of lunatic notion was that, anyway? That was the kind of thing crazy people thought, the kind of radioactive rumination that would leak through the cracks of a diseased mind. He pictured a legion of Day-Glo miniature skeletons scuttling through the crooks and eddies of his gray matter, planting seeds of insanity, and shuddered. It was padded room thinking. Straitjacket insight. Any rational person could see the black stretch of backwoods highway looked much more like the back of some monstrous hell snake. The asphalt did sort of remind him of scales more than concrete.

Ride the snake...

Rick shuddered again.

"I sort of want to hear The Doors."

Danny shrugged. "No Doors on the Zune." The musical portion of the evening's entertainment was courtesy of Danny's Zune. The MP3 player was connected to an adapter in the Chevelle's tape deck, and contained nearly 80 GB of Danny Spillane's favorite tunage. Everything worth hearing was on the goddamn thing. Motorhead, the Ramones, AC/DC. The Who, the Stones, Led Zeppelin. The Sex Pistols, Deep Purple, and Frank Sinatra. Bob Marley and Frank Zappa. The Pixies and Big Black. A shitload of Johnny Cash. Danny's taste was pretty damn eclectic.

So...

"I can't believe you don't have any Doors on the fucking Zune."

"Well, I don't have any Doors on the fucking Zune."

Rick shook his head. "Fuck."

A moment passed. The only sounds were the hiss of tires on asphalt and the clamor of conflicting weird impulses and theories in his head. Decidedly non-mainstream notions about the first moon landing and the assassinations of Marilyn Monroe and Paul Wellstone. Except that these didn't produce actual audible sounds. Or did they? Hold on now. Wait. Nope. That was all in his head. Jesus, that was freaky. He thought maybe he should snort some more coke. No. He wanted to get mellow again.

"Are we out of beer?"

Danny shrugged. "Might still be some in the back." He frowned. "Any idea where we are?"

"Nope."

"Huh. Guess I'll just keep going this way then."

"Whatever."

Rick twisted in his seat and peered into the back, looking for beer.

And that's when he saw her.

The dead bitch.

Rick's second scream that night was louder than the one that woke Danny.

PART TWO: THE DEAD BITCH

The revelation that they were riding with a non-breathing extra passenger caused Rick to fall backward and crack his back against the dashboard. He pointed at the back seat and gibbered unintelligibly for several moments.

Danny looked at him, his expression remarkably similar to the look you sometimes saw on the faces of tourists upon being accosted by deranged street people. Wary and with a hint of pity. "Um...could you maybe stop whining like a bitch for a minute and tell me what the fuck your damage is?"

One last squeal caught in Rick's throat, died there. He cleared phlegm from his throat and turned his pale face toward Danny. "You're going to want to pull over. Right now would be a good time."

Danny frowned. "Yeah? Why?"

"Because you're probably gonna want to get rid of the fucking gorgeous but also very fucking dead woman in the back of your car."

Danny didn't reply immediately.

He locked eyes with Rick, took a moment to appraise the subterfuge-free look of somber sobriety, saw that his friend wasn't pulling his leg, and promptly freaked the fuck out, unleashing an impressive scream of his own as he wrenched the Chevelle's steering wheel hard to the right and slammed on the brakes. They came to a skidding stop on the road's shoulder. Danny shifted in his seat and peered into the back.

He screamed again.

Rick and Danny locked gazes again.

They screamed some more.

"Oh, shit!"

"Oh, fuck!"

"What are we gonna do? What're we fucking gonna do?"

Rick stared at the dead woman. It was real obvious she was

totally fucking dead. No pulse check was necessary. Nor was the administration of CPR, or a desperate search for the nearest emergency room. The giant, ragged gash in her throat made that abundantly clear. She was dead. Lights out, sayonara, see ya fuckin' later. But that left a bigger mystery to consider. Several of them, actually.

Including.

Who the fuck was this dead fucking bitch?

Who the fuck killed her?

And why was she in Danny's fucking car?

For starters.

Rick looked at his friend. "Danny, man...you didn't kill this chick, did you?"

Danny managed to sneer and look hurt at the same time. "What the fuck kind of monster do you think I am?"

Rick nodded. "Yeah." He heaved a big breath and reluctantly looked at the dead bitch again. Christ, that big bloody hole. His stomach knotted. "Didn't think so, bro, but kinda had to ask."

Danny's shoulders sagged, and he nodded wearily. "Yeah. Guess so. And I guess you didn't kill her?"

Rick thought about it. It didn't seem likely. Brutal murder wasn't his bag at all. He didn't even like to step on insects, normally. And he sure didn't remember killing anybody tonight. Then again...he searched his memory...what little of it was available to him from the last several hours. He remembered drinking at various bars in Nashvegas over the course of several hours. Hanging with those chicks they met at the Gold Rush. Pretty young things. College girls. The dead bitch hadn't been one of them, he was pretty sure. Things from later in the evening got fuzzier. Flashing images of dancing girls and strobe lights. Standard nightclub activity. Then things got even fuzzier. More dancing girls, except this time they were naked and strutting across a stage. And after that, he could recall nothing else.

He frowned.

The dead bitch was kind of tall, maybe a few inches under six feet. She had long bottle-blond hair, plump red lips, heavily rouged cheeks, a slender but shapely build, and two buoyant breasts that looked unnaturally large. Those tits were really something else, the kind stand-up comics would make flotation device jokes about.

Could the dead bitch have been a stripper?

The fact that she wore only a G-string and heels that were several inches higher than strictly necessary struck him as a possible clue.

"I can think of only one possibility."

Danny was nodding as he said this. "Already there. We hooked up with Gypsy Rose there at the Sin Den. Made some kind of private arrangement. She came out to the car to take care of us. We were kind of smashed by then."

Rick snorted. "Yeah. Kind of."

"So she comes out to the car. Sees we're, I dunno, fucking passed out, and sees an opportunity. Might as well rip us off. How will we ever know? Who would we ever tell? Not the management. Not the cops. It would be the perfect petty fucking theft. But, while she's in the process of ripping us off—"

"—some other dude comes along."

Rick nodded again. "Some fucking lowlife."

"That part of town, I can definitely see it."

"He sees what she's doing. He's another opportunist. He kills her. Takes our money. Slips away into the night."

Rick shook his head. "And leaves us with one dead fucking bitch."

They stared at the dead bitch in contemplative silence for a while.

Then Rick said, "You really think that's what happened?"

Danny shrugged. "Dunno. Maybe one or both of us did it in the midst of an alcoholic blackout. But I think I'll stick with theory number one, if you don't mind."

Rick shivered. "Fine with me."

"But we're left with the question of what to do about her."

"That I've already got figured out."

"Tell me."

PART THREE: DEAD BITCH RISING

Getting her out of the car was not a pleasant task. Before they even attempted it, they argued heatedly over who would get the feet end and who would get the yucky throat-slit end. They settled the question by flipping a quarter. Danny called tails. He lost. They went for two out of three. He lost again. He wanted to go for three out of five, but Rick wasn't having it.

"I won, fair and square. Stop being a pussy about it."

Danny grimaced, but a look of grim acceptance settled into his features. "Yeah. Okay. Let's do this."

They spent a few last moments steeling themselves for the sickening task ahead by chugging the last of the beers from a twelve-pack they'd had to retrieve from beneath the dead stripper's sprawled legs. Then they got on with it.

They'd been clumsily negotiating their way through the dark woods for less than five minutes by the time something of crucial importance occurred to Rick. "Huh. Just thought of something."

Danny cursed as he stumbled over a rock. The dead woman's limp wrists slithered free of his sweaty palms and the back of her head thumped on the forest floor. He cursed again, knelt over the body, and cringed as he again was forced to touch the dead flesh. He stood up, lifting her by the wrists again.

He looked at Rick. "What were you saying?"

Rick smiled, a strange expression for a man gripping the thin ankles of a dead stripper in the middle of a dark and unfamiliar landscape. "I'm not covered in blood. Neither are you."

Danny squinted at him, his expression conveying non-comprehension for a space of several seconds. Then his eyes slowly widened. "Motherfucker." The quiet epithet was invested with an odd combination of disbelief and dawning awe. He let go of the stripper's wrists again and looked down at himself. The dead woman's head cracked against a rock, but Danny was too busy patting his clothes to be disturbed by the grisly sound. He finished his self-inspection and lit up the forest with a radiant grin. "By God, you're right." He shook a clenched fist at the sky and let out an exultant cry. "YEAH! FUCK YEAH!" Then he laughed and, still grinning, looked at Rick again. "We didn't do it, man! We really didn't."

Rick was grinning, too, but now there were tears in his eyes.

Until this moment, he hadn't realized how much doubt some secret compartment in his psyche had harbored regarding his potential guilt. But now that was gone, as was the potentially permanent stain on his soul. He still had no idea what had really happened to the dead bitch. Maybe their original theory was closer to the truth than they knew. But it didn't really matter. All he cared about was this incontrovertible proof that he and his friend weren't mad dog killers.

He let go of the dead stripper's ankles and did a wild dance of unrestrained jubilation. Danny performed a similar dance. They whooped and thrust their fists toward the sky. Their behavior was much like that of very devoted sports fan who have just watched their favorite team score the winning touchdown in the Super Bowl. They had bucked the odds and come out on top, snagging victory from the jaws of defeat just when things looked their darkest. They were going to fucking Disneyworld!

The mood didn't sour until Danny tripped over an unseen vine and fell at an awkward angle. His left ankle came down with too much momentum behind it and too much weight coming down on top of it. There was an audible snap of bone and Danny hit the ground hard, his mouth tasting leaves and dirt before he rolled onto his back and howled in agony. He sat up and clutched at his left leg, looked at Rick, and howled again.

Rick's stomach did a slow roll. Bile touched the back of his throat. The joy consuming him only a moment ago died, displaced by a sick fear that left him shaking and on the verge of expelling the contents of his upset stomach. It wasn't fair. Wasn't right. How could something so fucked up have happened so quickly and so unexpectedly? They'd been so close to being free of this inexplicable nightmare situation, and here suddenly was this fresh layer of hell, a fucking mundane injury.

Danny managed to speak between quick, panting gasps. "Aw...fuck...dude. I broke...the fuck out of...my ankle. It looks..." Here he let out a whimper and grimaced. "Oh fuck. It looks like...like my foot's hanging by a fucking hinge. Oh, sweet Jesus." Another whimper as he rocked and clutched at his leg. "Oh. It hurts, Rick. Oh fuck, it hurts. Please...help me..."

Rick mentally berated himself.

Get your shit together! Help the man!

Rick nodded silent agreement with the inner voice, which sounded more than a little like the growling voice of his dead father. He took a few steps toward his friend, cringing as he eyed the injured limb. His stomach rolled again. Sweat broke on his brow. His throat bulged and he had to swallow bile again. The foot really did look as if it were hanging from a hinge. Christ. Looking at it was bad enough. He'd hate to be Danny right now.

"Look, man. Here's what we'll do. I'll help you up. You'll throw an arm around my shoulder, and we'll just sort of—"

Rick came to a dead stop.

His heart nearly did the same.

Something had grabbed his ankle, was holding it fast in a grip of steel. It was like being held in place by Superman.

This just can't be.

I mean, come on. No fucking way.

He glanced down, saw the dead bitch snarling at him, her teeth bared and glinting in the sliver of moonlight just visible through the canopy of trees.

"Oh...shit."

A rumbling, garbled sound emerged from the dead woman's mouth. Maybe she was trying to tell him something. But her vocal cords had been too damaged by whatever had been used to slit her throat for it to be intelligible.

Danny whimpered again. "What the fuck's going on over there?"

Rick swallowed a lump in his throat and felt his stomach flutter yet again. "I, uh...well..."

"Spit it out, man!"

"The thing is, you're not going to believe it."

"Fuck! Will you just tell me already?"

Rick swallowed hard again. The reanimated stripper's hand was moving up his leg now, cold fingers sliding inside his pants leg and slithering up his calf. He let out a whimper of his own. "We have a sort of...zombie situation."

A silent moment elapsed.

Then Danny said, "What?"

"I said, we have—"

The dead bitch sat up and growled at him.

Rick screamed.

Seeing the zombie, Danny screamed, too.

Rick tried to move away from her again, but she held him in place with astonishing ease and bared her teeth at him again, her milky-white eyes flashing in the moonlight. Her giant breasts trembled and jiggled as she got to her feet and pulled him into a clinch that was a mockery of a lovers' embrace. Her hands snaked around his back and moved up to his shoulders as she pressed tight against him. The crush of her ginormous breasts against his chest made it hard for him to breathe. Her fetid breath made him gag, and this time he was unable to hold back the bile that came rushing up his throat.

She bared her teeth again.

Her mouth dipped toward the beating pulse visible at his throat, hungrily seeking the tender flesh there.

Then Rick puked in her face.

PART FOUR: THE FINAL FUCKING CHAPTER

A spew of hot vomit splattered against the zombie stripper's face. The dead bitch's reaction was akin to that of a vampire being struck by holy water. She screeched and released him, reeling backward and stumbling awkwardly in her high heels. The thing lost its footing and landed hard on its ass. But this development provided only a brief respite. The dead bitch bounced back to her feet with a preternatural speed and grace, and stood hunched over and snarling at him, hands extended toward him like claws. She shook her blood-flecked blond hair, flipping it like a supermodel turning at the end of a catwalk.

Rick was struck by the way the moonlight made all that bare skin shimmer.

Fuck.

She looked sexy as hell—if you could get past the gaping hole in her throat, that is.

Danny said, "Are you just gonna fuckin' stand there and let her kill us both?"

Rick kept his gaze on the dead bitch and said, "She's a

zombie, dude. And you wouldn't believe how strong. So I'm kind of lost here. I'm open to suggestions, though."

Danny whined. "Christ, the fucking pain. Look, there's a gun in my trunk. A loaded .38. Its in my gym bag. Get it and shoot her in the fucking head, the way they do it in the movies."

Rick frowned. "Why do you have a gun in your gym bag?"

"WILL YOU JUST FOR CHRIST'S FUCKING SAKE GET THE FUCKING GUN!"

The seething exasperation in his friend's pain-seared voice provided the spur to action he needed. He spun on his heel and ran back toward the road. And as he ran, he tried not to think about how vulnerable turning his back on the dead bitch made him feel. Of course, it could be worse. He could be Danny. Ankle broken, lying helpless on the forest floor with a flesh-hungry zombie stripper only a few feet away. But he didn't want to think about that either. Not yet. Because Danny was right. This was their only chance. He had to be fast. Super fucking fast.

Within moments he burst through the line of trees at the side of the road, spotted the Chevelle some ten yards to his left, and streaked toward it. He grabbed the driver's side door handle, yanked, and screamed. Locked. He hurried to the other side. Same thing. He peered inside and saw Danny's keys dangling from the ignition. Frustration roiled inside him, a fire spreading to every nerve-ending. It was useless to wonder how they could have been so stupid. There wasn't time. A shrill scream from the woods emphasized that point. Rick scanned the ground next to the car, spied a large rock in the ditch beyond the road's shoulder, and quickly retrieved it. He hurled the rock through the driver's side window, and his hand was slipping inside even as the rain of glittering safety glass fragments was settling on the seat. Another scream, this one a pulsing ululation of pain, exploded from the woods as his fingers found the trunk latch. Rick popped the trunk, found the gun exactly where Danny said it would be, and hurried back into the woods.

It wasn't as dark as it had been only minutes ago. The first violet tinge of dawn had begun to brighten the sky. Rick experienced a few moments of hopeless, heart-pounding frustration as he thought he'd gone the wrong way.

Until he tripped over Danny and fell to the ground.

The .38 flew from his hand.

An open palm scraped against a rock as he smacked the ground, drawing blood. He rolled onto his back and stared at Danny.

Stared at his slack features.

At the terribly still eyes.

And at the open cavity that had once contained his intestines, half-devoured fragments of which were arrayed around the body of his dead friend.

Danny gaped in disbelief at the body for a moment.

Then the grief hit him, a welling of intense emotion that rocked him backward, sent him scooting away from the body until his back met the base of a thick tree. He sat there and stared in helpless, sick fascination at his deceased friend for a brief time. Then it occurred to him to wonder what had become of the dead bitch. She was nowhere in sight. Where had she gone?

He didn't have to wonder about it long.

Behind me!

That graveyard breath was unmistakable.

Rick surged to his feet, but before he could flee the dead bitch emerged from the shadows behind the tree and seized him by an arm. She pulled him close and wrapped him up in that same faux-lovers' embrace, only this time it was more exuberant. She hooked a leg around him and writhed against him. The push of her titanic breasts forced the air from him again and he struggled to breathe.

Fuck, he thought. *I'm being molested by a fucking zombie dead bitch!*

This went on for a time.

He even began to feel a mild arousal.

What the hell, right?

He was dead anyway. Might as well go with it.

Something happened.

The dead bitch twisted her head away from him and snarled. Then she was ripped from the embrace and Rick staggered backward. He felt woozy and his vision blurred. He gave his head a hard shake to clear the cobwebs and gaped at the sight of a reanimated, zombified Danny locked in a thrashing, savage battle with the dead bitch. They rolled on the ground and tore at each other with their fingernails. Strips of the dead bitch's flesh came away from her back as Danny raked at her.

Rick shivered.

And a glint of light on steel caught his eyes.

The .38.

He picked the gun up.

Approached the combatants.

Aimed carefully.

Fired.

And fired again.

The bodies of the zombies went still.

Danny stared at them for a long time. At first, he couldn't connect Danny's violated body with the man who'd been his best friend since childhood. Then a wash of memories assailed him. Forts built in the woods. Secret clubs formed with their other friends. The wild times as teenagers. The quiet sadness they never talked about as their other friends grew up and started families, became responsible. The subsequent total commitment to drugs and booze as the only way of life that made any sense to guys like them. And now this. One of them dead in some anonymous section of wilderness. Eviscerated. And here he was, smoking gun in hand, no idea what to do next. After a while, he turned and walked back out to the road.

He swept the glass fragments from the driver's side seat—barely noticing the sting of multiple cuts to his flesh—and slipped behind the steering wheel.

He stared at the road ahead.

It was almost full light out now.

The road was just a road.

Leading everywhere and nowhere, like always.

But maybe there was a monster lurking somewhere toward the horizon, after all.

Maybe a lot of them.

Rick switched the radio over to the AM dial, found a 24-hour news station.

An announcer's static-garbled voice told him some things

he'd already guessed at: "Washington has declared a national state of emergency. Citizens are being advised to stay in their homes until the crisis has passed. Again, the bodies of the dead are rising to attack the living. Authorities urge everyone to avoid contact with the dead. If you must engage a reanimated corpse, be advised that you must destroy the creature's brain to kill it. A team of top scientists is working around the clock to solve this problem, although at this time no one knows the cause of the uprising. Some theorize radiation from—"

Rick stopped paying attention.

It was weird how on some level he was completely unsurprised by this. As if somehow he'd always known it was going to happen, that it was inevitable.

He switched the radio back to the tape deck and picked up Danny's Zune. Scrolling through the list of artists, he stopped on one and laughed.

Tears welled in his eyes.

"You fucking liar."

He cued up "The End" by the Doors and pushed play.

After the song was over, he did the only thing he could think to do. He lifted the gun and put it to his head. He closed his eyes and spent a last few moments thinking of the good things in his life. Family and old friends. Fun times he'd had. The music he enjoyed. Yeah, there were some people and things he would miss. But the world was dying, and he didn't want to face that alone. He began to apply pressure to the trigger.

And a voice from the passenger seat said, "Don't be a dick."

Rick's finger eased off the trigger. He opened his eyes and lowered the gun, turned his head toward the source of the voice. "Um…"

Danny's ghost sat stretched out in the passenger seat, one arm propped on the door, that familiar smirk on his face. At least he appeared to be a ghost--he had that sort of glowing spectral transparency they often had in movies. A more rational part of Rick's mind reminded him that he had done a lot of drugs in his life, had in fact done a lot of drugs within just the last twenty-four hours, and so this could very well be a hallucination.

Danny chuckled and said, "I'm not a hallucination."

"Fuck, you can read my mind."

Danny shook his head. "Nah. It's just you're as transparent as I am in your own way. And Rick, seriously, you weren't really about to blow your brains out after listening to "The End", were you?"

"Well…"

Danny's smirk deepened. "My God, you really were gonna do it. Look, unless you're some kind of morose high school kid, that's just weak. Even then, it's weak."

Rick nodded. He set the gun down in the tray beneath the radio. "You're right."

"Damn right I'm right."

"So how is it I can see you?"

Danny shrugged. "Who knows, man? Maybe all the drugs you've done have opened receptors in your brain that are usually closed." He giggled. "The fucking doors of perception. You're probably gonna have to stay high as hell to keep me around."

Rick smiled. "Makes sense."

He fished a half-smoked joint from his shirt pocket and lit it with the dashboard lighter. He inhaled deeply and made like he was going to pass the joint to Danny.

Danny scowled. "Dude, I'm a ghost. Non-corporeal. Get it?"

Rick frowned. "Oh. Right."

"So you're gonna have to get twice as high for both of us."

Rick choked on another lungful of smoke, laughter wheezing out of him. "Yeah. Shit. Didn't think of that. Good point."

Danny shifted in his seat, clasped his ghostly hands behind his non-corporeal head. "What can I say? I'm a smart motherfucker. Now cue up some tunes. And not fucking "The End" again. Some good road tune. Then let's get mobile again. We've got us a goddamn zombie apocalypse to check out."

Rick picked up the Zune and scrolled through the selections until he found "Deep Purple's "Space Truckin'".

He clicked Play.

And made a sound meant to mimick Jon Lord's keyboards.

Danny unclasped his hands and played air drums.

In a few moments, the Chevelle was rolling on down the road.

SLUGGER

Walter Percy's wrinkled face was expressionless, a calm exterior that betrayed none of his inner rage. He had always been good at masking his true feelings, a dubious talent that had contributed greatly to the breakup of his marriage. He was nearly as adept at blocking out emotion as he had once been at playing The Game.

The Game was baseball, of course. And he loved it with an obsessive passion; it ruled his life, touching every facet of his existence. It was the only thing left that still held any real meaning for him.

Today was the home opener for the Rochester Red Wings, a triple A club in the Orioles organization, and he should have been happy. The hell of off season was over, spring training and its petty controversies all but forgotten. He was in a ballpark, as close to nirvana as he ever got.

But the fucking kids were ruining it for him.

They laughed at him, giggling wildly like fucking idiots, taunting him with rude remarks about his enormous girth. They were clean-cut teenagers, all-American in appearance, and drunk on grain alcohol and youth. Kids who would have been begging for his autograph had his career not come to such an untimely end.

Instead, they were throwing paper beer cups at him. Only one found its target, striking the bridge of his nose, and then falling into his lap. A small quantity of beer—mixed with a liberal dose of saliva—poured out of the cup, soaking the crotch of his jeans.

"Hey fatso!" one of the brats yelled, "You piss yourself?"

He knocked the cup away, and continued in his attempt to ignore the creaseless barrage of insults. There was a game to watch, after all. A good game. The bottom of the sixth inning was just getting under way, and the score was tied. Mike Jensen, Denver's premier power threat, was stepping to the plate. The crowd rose as one, a tidal wave of flesh, and booed in unison.

Except for the assholes Walter Percy was sharing this otherwise deserted section of the right field bleachers with. They had lost all interest in the game, finding the verbal abuse of Walter more worthy of their attention. This was sport of a decidedly crueler nature than baseball, and to their way of thinking, more fun.

His head rigid, motionless, Walter's eyes moved side to side in their sockets, scanning the immediate area for security guards; none were in sight. They were apparently content to focus their energies on problems in the more crowded areas of the park.

Ordinarily, he enjoyed sitting out here, isolated from everyone else, apart from all the bullshit and the swarming mobs of children. He could see the action on the field well enough, and he had his binoculars, after all. So rarely did anyone else ever sit out here, he had come to think of this remote section of the bleachers as a home away from home, his own personal property. This was the only place that made him feel everything was right with the world; it acted as a sanity buffer, an assurance that maybe things weren't really so bad, and maybe he could cope with life another six months, hell, maybe even make it through yet another dreary off season.

Now, though, these fuckin' little jerks were violating his space, defiling its sanctity. He was royally pissed off, but he knew any action on his part would just inflame them, make the whole situation even worse, if that was possible. If he could just concentrate on the game properly…

"Lardbucket!"

Goddamn! Just leave me alone, he thought. *Go pick on someone else, for Christ's sake!*

"Bet you need a fuckin' shovel to find your dick in all that shit, don't ya, lardbucket?"

One of the girls, a striking blonde, shouted, "How do you jerk off, blubberbutt? I know, you use a bulldozer to get to it and a crane to bop it."

The blonde's salvo was apparently the funniest thing the kids had ever heard; they dissolved into uncontrollable laughter, sounding for all the world like asthmatic hyenas.

Once it had subsided they were ready to resume the verbal strafing. Apparently impressed by her previous shot, the others deferred to the blonde. "You know, you're SOOO sexy, blubberbutt; there's just SOOO much of you. I bet you have to—"

Enough! There was just so much a guy could take, and he had just reached that point. "Fuck off, cunt."

This hushed them instantly; they seemed momentarily unable to believe that this thing—this gluttonous pig—had dared to strike back.

It didn't last.

"Maybe," one of the guys said, "I should just come over there and kick your fat ass."

He faced them squarely for the first time. "Why don't you just go ahead and try, you stupid little prick."

The one who had made the threat set down his drink, then stood. He was tall and well-conditioned, muscular like a weightlifter. Walter had looked like that once, many years ago. Back then, he wouldn't have felt fear facing a guy like this; now, though, fear was exactly what he was experiencing, and he didn't like it one damn bit. Suddenly, he was furioius at himself for having let himself go so badly; mental self-denial blocks he had spent years building unclogged in a matter of seconds. God, it didn't have to be like this! He *could* have kept himself in shape, and doing so, he could easily have dealt with an asshole like this. He shook with the fury of his self-hatred.

The weightlifter grinned. "Some tough guy, huh?" The others laughed. "You're scared shitless, aren't you, fatso?" The blonde giggled.

Walter stood, but not with any intention to fight this guy;

it was a fight he couldn't possibly win, and he knew it. He had decided to cut his losses and leave. He sighed, his heart heavy with sorrow. He instinctively sensed it would be a long time before he would come back. He wouldn't chance meeting these assholes, or others like them, again.

He turned away from them, and started walking towards the concrete steps that led to the vending area. He descended the steps as quickly as his massive frame allowed, moved rapidly through the vending area—waving off a scantily clad girl who wanted to sell him a program, and finally stepped out into the parking lot.

He scanned the lot for his grey Honda, squinting to see in the rapidly gathering darkness. It was, he knew, somewhere in the third row to his right. He began to move in that direction.

As he neared the car, he sensed the people behind him before actually hearing them. He didn't have to turn around to know it was the kids from the bleachers. He had no doubt they had some malicious intent in mind. They were like hunting dogs who refused to give up their prey's scent. *And that's what they are*, he thought, *animals*. He picked up his pace, knowing full well the effort would be for naught. They were younger and faster than him.

He didn't stand a chance.

A well aimed kick to the ass sent him sprawling on the pavement. His lungs expelled most of their air-supply upon his belly's contact with the ground. He breathed heavily, raggedly, desperately pulling in large gulps of air. His eyes watered, forming tears that spilled down each side of his nose.

"Get up."

It was the weightlifter; he recognized the voice immediately. He remained on the ground, unable to move; he still hadn't caught his breath.

"I told you to get the fuck up; I know even lardasses like you can hear, so do what I told you."

A girl laughed. The blonde. The one who had been the most vociferous and cruel of them all. A girl, for Christ's sake. What had the World come to? "I don't think he *can* get up," she said. "He's so heavy he can't even lift himself off the ground."

He heard the soft pad of running shoes on the pavement. Then the blonde was squatting beside him. His eyes looked up at her; she smiled down at him, and his mind reeled, unable to accept the reality of the situation. She was pretty, very nice-looking, a cheerleader type. She was the kind of girl all high school boys—and a lot of older men—fantasized about. But the eyes at the center of that face were filled with unfathomable hate. *Where did it come from?* he wondered. *What could possibly cause it?*

Her smiled shifted, the lips puckering; they parted, the mouth opened wide to expel a large wad of saliva. Spit splashed down his face, mingling with the tears. Fresh tears poured down his face. He began to sob.

They all laughed. One of the other girls said, "poor baby."

The blonde still wore that bland smile. She was like a Barbie doll come to life, emotionless, devoid of any real feeling. Except unadulterated hate. "Yeah," she said, "poor fat little baby; you deserve to be punished, little baby."

She stood, and he stared up at those long, sleek, tanned legs; fantasy-worthy legs. Entranced, he watched as one of them reared back, then swung forward, the foot connecting solidly with his chin. His teeth ground together, biting into the tip of his tongue. A tiny amount of blood trickled out the corner of his mouth.

The others joined her. Three stood on each side of him. "Guess you don't have to get up, after all," the weightlifter said, then kicked him in the side. He saw the blonde's pink running shoe swing toward his again, felt it connect, felt the imprint of its sole on his flesh. Soon, the others joined in, delivering a seemingly endless barrage of blows to his beleaguered body.

He began to pray for quick death.

Miraculously, though, they left him alive. Bored with the casual torture of the fat man, they left him—a bloody heap—on the pavement. His mind was numb, his body the same. Through the haze, he heard their soulless laughter, their talk of making a beer run.

Alive.

He couldn't quite believe it.

But something *did* die in Walter Percy that night; that essential flicker of genuine humanity that had kept him sane, basically good, decent.

It was just gone.

Like it had never existed.

He had been called "Slugger" once, a long time ago, back in his days as the prime prospect in the New York Yankees minor league organization. Scouts had him pegged as the second coming of Mickey Mantle; he hit monstrous home run shots that inspired awe in all who saw them. Aside from his hitting prowess, he was a graceful ball-handler—scooping up grounders and snagging line drives with effortless ease—and he could scorch the base paths. He had been a sure thing, a can't-miss prospect on a fast track to the majors.

Life had been so simple then, uncomplicated; he knew what he was all about, where he was going, and what he would do when he got there. He saw everything in simple terms, in shades of pure white and pitch black; delineations between concepts of right and wrong were easily discerned, such as his impulsive decision to marry Louise after signing his first minor league contract.

In those days Louise was a pliable woman, and she had accepted his proposal immediately. They honeymooned in New York, visiting Yankee Stadium three straight days, knowing it would one day reverberate with the cheers of his adoring fans.

Those dreams were short-lived, however; two years later—just days after their anniversary—he collided with an opposing team's second baseman. His right knee was blown out, rendered useless; it would take years of rehabilitation before it would work right again.

His purpose in life taken away, he became a shell of a man, a mere husk. He compensated for the void in his soul by constantly filling his body with food, all manner of snacks and junk. Louise complained, bemoaning the ruination of his once Adonis-like physique. His body swelled, especially his belly; the once washboard-flat stomach now quite effectively hid his feet from view; their marital problems grew exponentially.

He was served with divorce papers on the day of their ninth wedding anniversary. The timing didn't faze him in the least; he was way past the point of caring. He knew she had been with other men lately, but that didn't matter. He *wanted* her gone; she was just a symbol of his shattered past, the broken dreams that could never be mended.

That was ten years ago. The intervening time had been uneventful. He worked at a gas station, earning just enough money to pay his rent and keep him well stocked in Twinkies and poptarts. In his free time he watched baseball on the cable superstations. He went to see the Red Wings whenever they were in town. He made a once a year trip to New York to see the Yankees play. During the off season, he kept track of the winter league, subscribing to the newsletters of each team.

Year after year his life followed this monotonous pattern. The monotony comforted him, nurtured him, kept him contented. As long as life followed rigid, set patterns he could deal with it.

Now, though, that was all over; the incident in the parking lot the previous night had changed everything. He was sick of the passivity with which he dealt with things. He wanted to feel *alive* again, strong, the way he had felt when he had been playing The Game. God, that seemed like a lifetime ago; he felt separate from the past, like it was something that had happened to another person entirely. He certainly bore little resemblance to that person; his ball-player incarnation would have kicked the shit out of those kids.

He wanted to be that person again.

He swung the new wooden bat with all the force he could muster, cutting a smooth arc through the still night air. At first, the bat had felt alien in his grip, its potential power untappable, but that didn't last. He was surprised at how quickly the old instincts returned. His swings were fluid, the uppercuts clean. He pictured himself hitting stinging line drives.

He was in a park, a recreational area with one crude playing field. He had spied it driving by earlier. It was dark, and no one was around; it had been too tempting to resist. He had stood out here at home plate, his new bat in hand, taking cut after cut at imaginary sliders, curveballs, and high velocity fastballs. He had even made one aborted attempt at rounding the bases, giving up midway between first and second. He would have to shed several dozen pounds before being able to accomplish something like that. His resolve to do so was implacable.

But it was getting late; time to go. He sighed, then took one final swing, creaming an imaginary Roger Clemens fastball over Fenway's Green Monster.

He turned away from the playing field, and began to make his way back toward the car, trudging through tall, unmown grass. As he neared the roadside, he noticed a young man in a jogging suit walking along the sidewalk. The man was short of breath, apparently having worn himself out after a long sprint. The man came to a complete stop, bent over, placed his hands on his knees, and breathed deeply.

He's definitely winded, Walter thought, approaching him. He held the bat loosely in his right hand, rocking the handle between thumb and forefinger.

The man looked strong, conditioned. He reminded Walter of the weightlifter at the ballpark. His right hand tightened around the handle as he came up behind the man; the left hand took its place beneath the right, bringing the bat into position.

Sensing danger a moment too late, the man whirled around. His mouth opened, and he gaped at the huge man with the big stick.

Walter smiled. He couldn't have asked for a better angle. The man's head was like a hanging curveball, a home run invitation offered up on a silver platter. He brought the bat around, driving the fat end into the man's astonished face. The crack of bone beneath the force of wood was immensely satisfying; it was as though he had gotten the meat of the bat on a Nolan Ryan heater and had thoroughly demolished it.

It felt good.

Real good.

Like being reborn.

Later, sitting in the car, he cleaned the blood off the bat with a towel. He whistled "Take Me Out to the Ballgame."

He winked at the grinning trophy on the dashboard.

Game Ball.

God, he felt great! After a too lengthy stay on the disabled list, Slugger was back, revitalized and invigorated.

And he had a new game to play.

PIZZA FACE

Will Hopkins, pizza delivery guy extraordinaire, was on his last run of the night. He'd hit two of the three houses on the run already, and the last came into view as he rounded a bend on a residential road.

Hot damn, he thought, *almost quittin' time*.

He was already considering the array of post-work activities that awaited him upon his return to Casa Hopkins. First, and this was absolutely non-negotiable, he'd pop open a cold Old Milwaukee. Then he'd turn on the tube and hunt down something good and sleazy. Jerry Springer, maybe. Or maybe some soft-core porn on Skin-e-max.

Oooh, yeah...

But first he had to take care of business.

Will drove past the house, made a wide, looping turn in the dark cul-de-sac just past the house, and pulled to a stop at the curb next to the mailbox.

His headlights briefly illumined the back of a van before he clicked them off.

The house was the only one on the street with lit windows. Not too many people were up late in a neighborhood like this. These were working-class people. Responsible people with mortgages and bills to pay. Will supposed he was doomed to one day inhabit a house just like this one. He would have a non-exciting job that required him to get up at an ungodly hour. He would have a reasonably attractive—but not beautiful—wife and a kid or two.

Will sighed.

It was depressing.

He didn't want to be an 'average Joe'.

He lifted the pizza off the passenger seat, swung the driver's side door open, and got out. The strap-on Pizza Zone sign glowed dimly atop the roof of his Toyota hatchback. The cool night air felt good. A gentle breeze ruffled his shaggy hair as he walked down the driveway toward the house.

He ascended some steps to the front porch, jabbed the doorbell, stepped back, and waited for the door to open.

He heard muffled movement beyond the door. A clomp of footsteps, something that sounded like a beanbag hitting a floor, and a metallic rattle that might have been keys rattling on a ring. Or a big pile of dishes shifting in a sink. Or cutlery clinking in a tray. Knives and forks and spoons.

Will frowned.

He took an unconscious, shuffling step back to the edge of the porch. His stomach had that funny, fluttery feeling he got when something didn't feel right. But he was in a nice neighborhood. Some boozed-up redneck wasn't about to open the door and start giving him shit. This wasn't a goddamn trailer park. Nor were there any predators prowling the well-lighted streets.

Well, probably not.

Shit, definitely not—there were too many other neighborhoods more conducive to the activities of petty criminals. Neighborhoods that Pizza Zone, thank God on his almighty fucking throne in heaven, didn't service.

He heard more movement from inside the house.

The footsteps again, booted feet, getting louder for a moment, then receding, followed by a dimmer sound of something sliding across a floor.

Will breathed an exasperated sigh. "Jesus," he muttered. "What are they doing in there, moving furniture? Come on, peeps, I wanna go home."

The door stayed shut.

His mind turned again to the entertainment he had planned for the evening. He was pretty sure Skin-e-max was showing a double feature of Shannon Tweed psycho-slut-from-hell movies. Thinking about Shannon Tweed's breasts fueled his impatience, and he stepped forward to jab the doorbell again.

Then, for good measure, he banged on the door with the base of a fist.

Tell me you didn't hear that, fuckers.

The entreaty escalation produced immediate results.

Will heard the unmistakable sound of a deadbolt being thrown back. Then there was a slow grinding sound—metal sliding against metal—as the brass doorknob turned to the left. The doorknob stopped turning, there was a freeze-frame moment of stillness, then the door edged away from the doorjamb.

Will summoned forth his brightest customer-kiss-ass smile and said, "Pizza Zone!"

But the door only opened a crack. The minute opening revealed only darkness. Someone had turned the lights out. He experienced a recurrence of the fluttery feeling in his stomach. Something funny was going on here.

Hushed voices emanated from the other side.

A guy and a gal.

Will grinned.

Because suddenly he knew what the deal was. What we have here, pimps 'n' bitches, is a classic case of coitus interruptus.

He grinned, suddenly feeling a need to make mischief.

I'm a naughty boy.

"Yo, what's up in there? Didn't you hear me? Your. Pizza. Is. Here." Will said the last bit slowly, as if he were addressing an assembly of special-needs children. "Hell-low-oh?"

The door edged another inch away from the door. An eye appeared through the crack. The eye was blue and belonged to a girl. He didn't need to see the rest of her to deduce that. The subtle smudge of eye shadow gave that away.

Then he heard the girl's voice, a sibilant whisper: "Go away!"

The door creaked.

It was closing.

Will acted without thinking. He jammed a foot through the narrow opening before the door could finish closing. The girl continued to apply pressure to the door, compressing the white

Reebok and making his foot hurt. Balancing the pizza on the upraised palm of his left hand, he halted the door's progress with the splayed palm of his right hand.

The girl's voice came again: "Go away!"

Louder now, exuding frustration and...what?...fear?

Of what?

"Hey, chill, okay? I'm not a robber. I'm not a rapist. I'm not any kind of bad guy. I'm just a dude with a job to do."

The girl breathed a sigh of surrender. "I gave you a chance, mister. It ain't my fault, ya hear?"

Will's brow furrowed.

Well, this is odd.

"What's not your fault, baby doll?"

A man's voice spoke next. "This, motherfucker."

Then the door was standing open, and a behemoth of a man filled the doorframe. Two beefy hands seized handfuls of Will's Pizza Zone golf shirt and pulled him inside. His assailant spun around, planted his feet, and launched him into the air.

The pizza box flew away from him, a colorful blip winking in the darkness.

Will glimpsed a blur of motion behind the hulking shape of the man.

The girl, a slender babe with dark hair and big boobs, was closing the front door.

It slammed shut at the exact moment Will's back collided with an ornate grandfather's clock. The collision hurt like a mofo. Clattering chimes filled his head with dissonant, anarchic music, little clusterbombs of sound that blotted out any capacity for coherent thought for several moments.

He tumbled away from the clock, then pitched forward with his hands outstretched. His hands met resistance, something solid—the glass door of a curio cabinet that stood opposite the still-reverberating grandfather's clock. He experienced a moment of perfect clarity, a nanosecond during which his brain analyzed the situation, came to a conclusion about what was going to happen, and informed him there was nothing he could do about it.

His hands pushed through the glass.

He cried out as broken shards sliced up his forearms.

And he kept falling, still powerless to halt his body's momentum. He plunged through the curio cabinet, his shoulder struck a shelf, and he dropped to his knees.

Blood rolled in rivulets down his arms.

Fragments of glass tumbled off his back and cracked on the floor.

Will wanted to cry.

The pain was immense.

He was reminded, however, of what his mother used to say in times of great stress (such as when the cocaine fund ran low and she was forced to replenish it with money diverted from his college fund): Be thankful for the little things, sonny.

Will heeded his mother's words now.

He was thankful for the moment of stillness. He was certain it was to be short-lived, but he was thankful nonetheless. His breath was coming in ragged gasps. A drop of something that might have been sweat—but was probably blood—swelled at the tip of his nose. He watched it fall away and hit the hardwood floor with a wet plip.

Yep, he thought, *that's blood.*

He looked up to see his attacker looming over him.

The man was enormous, but that wasn't the most disconcerting element of his appearance. He wore shiny leather pants, black combat boots, and nothing else. His thighs were as big around as oak trees. He was bald, bare-chested, and more muscular than anyone Will had seen outside of a wrestling arena. A big, distended belly drooped over his belt. A powerfully-built, beer-guzzling psycho motherfucker from hell.

Will felt his balls shrivel.

But the most surreal aspect of the man's countenance was his well-tended Fu Manchu mustache—well, that or his lack of eyebrows.

Goddamn, Will thought, what kind of freak shaves his eyebrows?

But he didn't have time to ponder the question any further. Chrome Dome again seized handfuls of his shirt and yanked him to his feet.

Will's head flopped about on his shoulders.

He didn't know what the dude had in mind, but he was pretty sure it wouldn't be pleasant. He mentally braced himself to board another flight of Air Hopkins.

But that didn't happen.

Instead, the man relinquished his hold on Will's shirt. "Goddamn." He looked Will up and down. "What kinda get-up is that?"

Will blinked moisture out of his eyes, and his head stopped spinning long enough to allow his brain to compose coherent sentences. "It's a Pizza Zone get-up. I work for Pizza Zone. I deliver pizzas. That's my job. I take pizzas to people who want pizzas. So, look, if you changed your mind about the pizza, you could've just said so."

Chrome Dome was still scowling. "And what's that on the end of your nose." He squinted and leaned closer. Then he burst out laughing. "It's a zit."

Will frowned. "Is not."

Chrome Dome cackled some more. "It's a giant, malignant-looking blackhead." Tears of hilarity leaked from the corners of his eyes. "Ha-ha! The pizza geek has a pizza face."

Will couldn't see his nose, of course, but he knew there was no zit there. "It's not a zit. It's blood. Are you blind?"

He heard the girl chuckle.

She sidled up next to the big guy.

Despite the direness of his predicament, Will was unable to resist the opportunity to ogle the girl. She was a curvy little thing. She wore tight blue jean cutoffs, a little half-shirt that just covered her jutting breasts, and nothing else. Will saw himself running a hand up a tawny thigh, up higher, moving outward with the sweet swell of her hip, then stopping to cup a handful of that delectable ass.

She was the most mouth-watering piece of girl-candy he'd laid his eyes on in some time.

Her full, pouting lips looked custom-made to provide oral pleasure.

The lips turned up a barely perceptible notch. "He's sorta cute, Hank."

Hank scowled. "Shut up, you horny slut." He clubbed Will

upside the head. "Stop checkin' out my bitch, asshole."

A fresh blast of agony squashed Will's libido.

The world went away for a moment, then came back blurry.

"Oh..." He groaned, feeling a tickle of bile at the back of his throat. "Oh, man...I think I'm gonna be sick."

Hank laughed. "That's the least of your worries, pizza face. And it is too a zit. Looks ready to burst." His face screwed up in disgust. "Dude, it's pretty gross."

Will opened his mouth to retort, but Hank was done arguing—he pushed Will through an archway into the home's living room.

The lights were out here, too, but the flickering screen of a large television provided some illumination. Enough illumination to confirm Will's darkest fears. The room was tastefully decorated. There were two plush sofas, a big recliner, and an oak coffee table with glass insets. Real Martha Stewart stuff. Two hairy guys who looked like bikers occupied one of the sofas. They wore leather chaps over blue jeans, big shitkicker boots, and denim vests over black t-shirts. Their bulging biceps and forearms were profusely tattooed.

Another girl was curled up in a recliner. A blond babe every bit as tasty as Hank's girl—in that cheap slut sort of way.

Will was sure these people were not the legal residents of the house.

They fell into a category one might generously label "uninvited guests".

The people who called this once-idyllic slice of suburbia home were present, though. To Will's left was a kitchen with a long, white-tiled island and an L-shaped counter with a gas-powered stove. A man's severed head sat in a pan atop a burner. A headless body lay sprawled next to the island. It wore a robe that hung open to reveal a torso punctured by numerous knife thrusts. The TV screen glowed brighter for a moment, and Will saw that there was a tremendous amount of blood.

Splashes of coagulating crimson on the island tiles.

Dark pools of deep red on the floor.

The woman of the house was still alive. Will got a good look at her when he jerked his gaze away from the grisly tableau.

She was a good-looking brunette in her late-thirties. A sexy silk nightie that barely reached the tops of her thighs made her look like a Victoria's Secret model. She was prone on the floor in front of the TV, with a gag in her mouth and her hands and feet bound with duct tape.

Hank slammed the base of a palm into Will's back, driving him farther into the room.

"Have a seat, pizza face, so's we can sort this out."

Will stumbled forward on legs that felt shot full of novocaine. He stepped past the smirking bikers and settled into the empty sofa. Hank stepped into the middle of the room, impeding the view of the TV.

One of the bikers groaned. "Aw, Hank, you're blockin' our view of the fat lesbos on Jerry Springer."

Hank directed a malevolent glare at the insolent biker. "Shut up, Spike. We've got some serious business to discuss." He eyed each of the assembled scumbags in turn, allowing them long moments to feel the fury emanating from him.

They squirmed.

Hank was the obvious leader of this gaggle of wackos.

They feared him.

Will felt a mad impulse to laugh.

Shit, you'd have to be a goddamn moron not to fear Hank.

That, or the Terminator.

"I'm gonna ask a question, and I don't want any bullshit. Which one of you stupid meth-heads thought it'd be a good idea to order a pizza right smack in the middle of a home invasion?"

Silence.

The bikers and the blond girl squirmed some more, fearing the sure-to-be-terrible wrath of their inquisitor.

Hank was seething. "Answer. Me. Now." The veins on his bald scalp stood out, his eyes bulged, and his nostrils flared. His voice was low and hoarse, almost demonic. "I'm going to kill all of you if I don't get an answer."

The blond girl huffed. "J-Dog did it."

'J-Dog' was apparently the other biker. He shot an angry glare at the blond. "You lying bitch!" He jabbed a forefinger in her direction and turned his distraught face up toward Hank.

"She did it, man! I swear ta fuckin' God, Hank!"

Hank shook his head. "You idiots." He put a hand to his temple, closed his eyes, and appeared to work at summoning a level of calm. His eyes snapped open again. "I guess I don't care who did it. What's done is done. However, we're left with a dilemma."

Spike frowned. He looked confused. "Whuh...what's a duh...duh-lemmer?"

Hank said, "A conundrum."

Spike's frown deepened. "A condom...drum?" Then his face brightened, and he smiled. "Like a barrel o' rubbers, huh?"

Hank lifted Spike off the sofa, placed him in a headlock, and laughed as the biker thrashed uselessly in his grip.

The blond shrieked. "Don't hurt my baby!"

Hank snapped the biker's neck.

The body tumbled to the floor, where it twitched a time or two before going still.

The blond squealed.

She slid off the recliner, knelt over the dead biker, and turned a tear-streaked, beseeching face up toward Hank. "Whuh-whuh...why?"

Hank shrugged. "Nobody that stupid deserves to live."

Will thought, *This is one harsh dude*.

His gaze went to the woman in the nightie.

She was looking at him, her eyes wide and full of terror.

Eyes that communicated desperation.

Supplication eyes.

Will looked away, unable to bear the woman's imploring gaze a moment longer.

Hell, what could he do for her?

He couldn't even help himself.

Hank seized a fistful of the blond's hair, hauled her to her feet, and dumped her back in the recliner. "As I was saying, we're faced with a dilemma. Pizza face has seen some shit we can't let him talk about."

J-Dog said, "So? We just waste his ass, right?"

Will gulped.

Hank's girl entered the living room.

She was carrying the pizza box.

She caught Will's eye, smiled, and walked over to him.

Will liked the way her hips moved.

She sat down next to him, folded her legs beneath her, and leaned toward him. "Want a slice?"

She opened the box.

The top flap covered his lap.

Which was good, because he didn't want Hank to get a glimpse of the woody he was sporting. The girl's bare knees were pressed against his thigh, and his vantage point allowed him an unobstructed view of the tops of her breasts. The plunging neckline of the half-shirt displayed them in a way that made his mouth go dry.

She removed a slice of pizza from the box.

Wedged it into her open mouth.

She chewed lustily, slurping in dangling strands of cheese like noodles.

Hank helped himself to a piece, too. "Yeah, we could waste him." He wolfed down the slice like a starving animal in the wild. He smacked his lips and belched. "But then he'd never get back to the pizza place. The other pizza bitches would start worrying about him. Pretty soon we'd be ass-deep in cops."

Nobody said anything for a while. Will surreptitiously scanned their faces. They all seemed to be deep in thought, a process that looked more problematic and painful for J-Dog and the blond. Hank was the only one who maybe had an IQ beyond the double-digit range. And he was pure-ass crazy.

For the first time, Will began to consider the prospect of his death as an imminent event. He supposed that'd been the case from the beginning, but he was only now fully conscious of the reality of it. There'd just been too much else going on, too many grotesque revelations for his brain to process.

Now, however, the likelihood of his own death displaced all other concerns.

What would it be like?

Would it hurt?

He considered the severed head in the frying pan, then willed the vision away, because the answer to his question was plainer than a blackhead on a teenager's nose: Yep, it's gonna hurt. It's gonna hurt like a sumbitch.

He realized he was shaking, but he was powerless to quell his body's involuntary reaction to possible death by dismemberment.

And what did it really matter?

Shit, he wasn't supposed to show fear?

He could only hope they wouldn't take their time snuffing him.

Better to die fast and relatively easy.

A litany of prayers started running through his head: Please, God, forgive me for my sins. I haven't been such a bad guy. Sorry I knocked over my goldfish bowl that time I was stoned. I loved that fish, man. I didn't mean to kill him. And I'm sorry about the porn. I know I watch a lot of it. I know it's sinful. There's just something about lesbian porn, ya know? But I'm sorry, I know it was wrong. The body is a temple. I shoulda been more respectful of the holy creation that is Woman. Ahh... oh, hell, I'm just sorry, sorry as can be, God.

Hank was scowling at him.

Will blinked. "Uh...was I saying any of that out loud?"

His girl giggled. "I like all-girl porn, too."

Will's face reddened. "Er..."

Hank made a noise of disgust. "Stop flirting with the dead-meat, Starlene."

Starlene mimicked the noise he'd made. "I ain't flirtin' with the boy, Hank. I'm just havin' some fun with him. I like messin' with 'em before you kill 'em, you know that."

Some of the tension drained out of Hank's face. He nodded. "Yeah, I know you do, hon. You just get a little too into it sometimes, worries me."

Her lower lip puffed out. "Baby, you know I only got eyes for you." She spoke in a tone of mock-hurt. "Don't you know how much I love you?"

Hank grinned. "Shit, yeah, I know that."

He reached into a pocket of his leather pants, removed a long folding knife, and snapped open a gleaming blade. Will's shaking worsened as the big man approached the sofa.

This is it, he thought.

He pictured the blade punching into his throat.

Pictured blood jetting out of the opening.

But Hank didn't stab him.

He took hold of one of Starlene's hands, folded the knife handle into it, and kissed the back of the hand. "You keep an eye on pizza face, baby. I gotta take me a shit."

Starlene's eyelids fluttered. "Baby, you're so romantic."

He smiled, then he kissed her on the mouth and was gone.

The room's occupants remained silent until they heard a door close in another room.

The blond let out a big breath. "He's outta control, Star."

Will watched the good humor seep out of Starlene's face. "I know, y'all."

J-Dog said, "I hate to speak ill of ol' Hank, but he's scarin' me. The way he killed Spike..." He shook his head. "That was plain uncalled for."

Will wanted to say, "Oh, yeah? Unlike the guy with no head, eh?"

But he kept his mouth shut.

The blond said, "So whatta we do about it?"

Starlene sighed. "Dunno. I'm thinkin'."

Well, this was an interesting development. Hank didn't have his followers as cowed as they allowed him to believe. He was just a room away, and they were in here plotting his undoing. A flicker of hope flared to life inside him.

"Um...why..." He paused to clear his throat. "Sorry, I'm scared shitless. Why don't you guys just ditch him?"

They seemed to roll their eyes as one.

Starlene said, "Because he wouldn't rest until he'd tracked us down and killed us. He is absolutely unrelenting, a fucking human killing machine."

Will's eyes became narrow slits. "Say...what happened to the cornpone accent?"

She grunted. "An act. I want him to underestimate me."

"I'll be damned."

The blond chuckled. "Her name ain't Starlene, either."

'Starlene' glared at her. "Too much information, Crystal."

"Sorry."

The muffled sound of a toilet flush emanated from the distant bathroom.

The brunette said, "Hush, everybody."

Hank ambled back into the room. He seemed more relaxed, less manic than he'd been prior to moving his bowels. He rubbed a hand over his crotch. "I don't know about you, J-Dog, but my tractor's about ready to plow some new fields."

J-Dog chuckled.

The chuckle sounded forced to Will's ears; then again, Hank hadn't been privy to the mutinous conversation, so he probably didn't pick up on the subtlety of tone.

The brunette said, "Hank, goddammit, I thought you was my man. Now you're gonna fuck that wrinkly ol' wifey-poo bitch." She harrumphed. "Ain't right, baby, ain't right at all."

Hank stared at her.

The stern expression on her face wilted.

"No more lip from you tonight, Starlene. I'm warning you."

He lifted the bound woman off the floor.

"Excuse me, girls, I've got business to attend to." He leered at the brunette, then his gaze slid toward J-Dog. "Come on, J, let's show this hoochie mama a good time."

J-Dog rose slowly from the sofa. "Sure thing, Hank."

There wasn't much enthusiasm in his voice.

Hank glared at his girl again. "You and Crystal watch the pizza bitch whilst me and my amigo make proper use of the master bedroom."

Hank took their silence for acquiescence.

He walked past the sofa on his way out of the room.

Later, when the burst of adrenaline had faded and the violence of the moment was over, Will would try to remember whether there'd been any conscious formulation of a plan on his part.

Not that it mattered.

Only the results were important.

What he did was simple—he extended a foot as Hank walked by, and the big man pitched forward, the nightgown-clad woman spilling out of his arms. It was an awesome sight, like watching a mountain collapse.

Will liberated the knife from the brunette's hand before she knew what was happening. He moved with a speed surpassing anything in his experience.

One moment he was on the sofa.

The next moment the knife was in his hand and he had a knee planted squarely in the middle of Hank's back.

A fraction of a moment later the blade was buried to the hilt in Hank's neck.

Hank spasmed.

Tried to rise.

Will yanked the knife out and put it in him again, this time through the ear.

He gave it a twist and yanked it out again.

The knife rose and fell several more times. Hank was dead after the first few thrusts, but Will wasn't inclined to stop butchering the behemoth's body. Adrenaline was part of it, but the murderous fury was also fueled by paranoia, by a conviction instilled by a lifetime of watching bad movies on late night TV.

He imagined Hank rising from the dead like Jason Voorhees.

Crazy.

Thing was, Will could just see it.

It would be a defiance of reality every bit as absurd as the notion that he'd managed to successfully vanquish the monster that was Hank.

So he kept stabbing him.

After a while, he rolled the big body over and stared at the dead man's unseeing eyes.

A chilling sight.

But then Will experienced another flash of inspiration.

He grinned. And he started cutting again.

Daylight.

The house and immediate vicinity was crawling with cops and evidence techs. The authorities had been summoned by the concerned night manager of a Pizza Zone restaurant. One of their delivery boys had gone out on a run last night and never returned.

Detective Mitch Roth suspected no one would ever see the

pizza boy again. He was officially missing, but he had a feeling his body would be discovered in a ditch or ravine sometime in the coming hours.

He leaned against the archway leading into the blood-splattered living room.

He was trying to stay out of the way of the evidence techs—Lord knew they had their hands full with this one.

He heard footsteps on the hardwood floor behind him.

Detective Cooper moved into his field of vision. "Looks like some shit out of The Texas Chainsaw Massacre."

Roth nodded. "Yeah, what they did to the one guy, the big one in the leather pants...you just don't want to believe people capable of sick shit like that are out there."

Cooper grunted. "You know they are, Mitch. The world's fulla scum."

One of the evidence techs gagged behind his mask.

Another tech leaned over his shoulder, grimaced at what he saw, and looked at the detectives. "You guys should see this."

Roth and Cooper exchanged wary glances.

Both men started moving toward the techs.

The first tech said, "Careful where you step. Stay off the marked areas."

Roth said, "So what is it?"

They were looking at a pizza box.

The lid was emblazoned with the familiar red and green Pizza Zone logo. Someone had scrawled PEEK-A-BOO across it in big letters with a marker.

A tech lifted the lid.

Cooper shuddered.

Roth could barely breathe. "Oh...Jesus..."

The remains of a barely-eaten pizza were at the bottom of the box. Stretched from crust to crust was something that resembled a mask.

Except it wasn't.

Cooper said, "It's the big guy's face."

There was more.

Two bloody orbs that had to be eyeballs had rolled into the corners of the box.

Roth couldn't suppress what happened next. He upchucked all over the box and coffee table, tainting a shitload of evidence and soiling his new suit.

He tendered his resignation later that afternoon.

Will Hopkins's body wasn't discovered in a ditch or ravine.

He was very much alive—more alive than ever, in fact.

He rode off into the night with 'Starlene' (whose real name turned out to be Nicole), Crystal, J-Dog, and a woman in a nightgown they jokingly re-named Patty.

As in Patty Hearst.

The gang had many adventures together in the coming years.

Will avoided the dreaded fate of a life in mundane suburbia.

And they all lived happily ever after.

The same could not be said for some of the people they encountered on the endless highways and byways of the land of the free.

REMORSE

Now that it was done he wished he could take it back. Now that the surge of adrenaline had passed and he was no longer in the heat of the moment, he wanted to roll back time and choose another course of action.

It wasn't possible, of course.

There was no 'Undo' button for bloody murder.

The blood-spattered cleaver slipped from Jack Roth's numb fingers and fell in a smooth arc toward the hardwood floor, where the exquisitely sharp blade embedded itself with an emphatic *thunk*.

Jack was alone in the room.

Now.

The only other humans in the room had recently ceased breathing. And dead people didn't count as company. Jack didn't know the guy's name, but he recognized him from the coffee shop down the street, Mondo Java, where he worked as a cashier. Lorene, Jack's now-deceased fiancee, was always raving about their lattes. Visits to Mondo Java were a long-established part of her daily routine.

Now, of course, Jack knew the attraction was about more than coffee.

Attraction he understood. That was something you could forgive. Monogamy didn't render a person blind. There was a place for benign, purely aesthetic appreciation of the opposite sex. But to take attraction one step further and betray the trust of a committed relationship just wasn't something he could let pass.

Still.

Probably he'd overreacted.

If things had gone according to the night's original schedule, he wouldn't be standing in the middle of this charnel house of a room with blood all over his nice clothes. He'd been set to spend the weekend in another city on business, but he'd only gotten as far as the airport lounge. Luke Riggins, a senior VP at his company, called Jack's cell number to inform him the scheduled round of meetings had been canceled. Jack, who'd been none-too-happy about spending yet another business weekend away from Lorene, decided not to call her.

He wanted to get a bouquet of roses and make a romantic, surprise return.

She'd been surprised, all right.

"Surprise" was a mild word for what Jack felt upon seeing Lorene and the coffee shop guy writhing about on the sofa in a state of partial undress. She'd been on her back, with the guy kneeling between her knees and fumbling with the clasps of her bra. When Jack opened the door to their penthouse apartment, the shirtless guy shrieked like a woman, grabbed his shirt, and began mumbling apologies as he headed for the door.

But loverboy never made it to the door.

Jack knocked him to the floor with one blow to the throat. Lorene opened her mouth to scream, but he moved to subdue her just as quickly. Then he went into the kitchen to get the cleaver.

And now Lorene and Mr. Java lay dead on the floor.

In pieces.

Lorene's head was in a flower pot on the coffee table.

Mr. Java had been posthumously castrated.

And Jack felt ill.

Very, very ill.

Not at all as he'd felt in the midst of creating the carnage before him. There had been no thought process involved in what happened, no conscious decision to kill and mutilate. He'd acted on brute instinct, blind rage consuming him as he butchered their flesh and wallowed in blood. The animal primitivism of the act had affected him another way, triggering an arousal that was only now beginning to fade.

But now he was shaking. His teeth chattered and he felt feverish, like a person coming down with the flu. Sweat streamed from his pores, gluing his starched white shirt to his back and armpits. He coughed and loosened his tie so he could breathe. Looking at the strewn parts of his dead love's body, he realized he'd crossed an important line, from human to monster.

Numbness gave way to sobs and tears.

He removed his tie and shirt and covered his face with his hands.

"Jesus, forgive me."

But Jack wasn't really a religious man. Beseeching Christ now was a pitiful joke. How could there be forgiveness for his awful deeds? He felt vile, like something gross you wipe off your shoe. Like fresh dogshit. The memory of the erection he'd sported while chopping Lorene's limbs off shamed him.

Jack had always considered himself a moral man, a good man. He'd gone out of his way to live right and treat others with respect and kindness. He'd never so much as raised a hand to a woman. Jesus Christ, he donated money to shelters for battered women every year! So he couldn't understand why he'd so easily surrendered to murderous fury. Maybe hitting the guy once would've been acceptable. It was what guys wanted to do when confronted with a situation like this.

But to kill him?

To kill Lorene?

To butcher them?

These were not the actions of a sane man.

How could he live with this?

Well.

The answer to that question, at least, was simple.

He *couldn't* live with it.

He thought again about his wish to take it all back. It didn't seem fair that a few minutes of unthinking violence should so irrevocably alter everything. He should be able to reverse this insanity. Erase the whole regrettable episode from his memory banks. Remembering his thought about life not having an 'Undo' button, he now thought a more desirable option would be a 'Reset' button, like the ones on video game systems—you used them when you didn't like the way the game was going and wanted to start over.

If there is a God, he thought, He needs to enter the goddamn digital age.

Come on, God, bestow upon humanity the miracle of the holy reset button!

Grief-choked laughter bubbled out of Jack.

And he thought, I'm going insane, yes I am, la de da de da.

"You're not insane, Jack."

Jack jumped at the sound of the other voice in the room.

"Okay, so maybe you flew off the handle here a bit, but you're not insane."

The voice was behind him.

Jack whirled around and gasped at the incongruous sight of a smirking, leather-jacketed thug leaning against a wall. The dark-complected man's shaggy hair was greasy and he had what looked to be a perpetual five o'clock shadow. He wore boots, faded jeans, and a t-shirt emblazoned with a picture of a beer bottle and the words "Salvation Ale". A halo and wings logo fluttered above the bottle.

Despite the substantial guilt he felt, Jack nonetheless panicked at the notion of a witness to his crime. The tip of his right foot nudged the embedded cleaver blade. Indignation flooded his senses, overwhelming the guilt and remorse. This person was an intruder in his home! He was violating Jack's privacy. He was a threat, a danger clear and present.

Jack knelt and pried the cleaver out of the floor.

The thug chuckled. "You really don't need to do that, Jack."

Jack snarled and leapt toward the intruder. The man just kept smiling as Jack bore down on him, and he didn't so much as flinch when the cleaver blade slammed into his shoulder.

Jack wrenched the blade out and whipped it around again, this time burying it in the grimy fuck's neck. The force of the blow was nearly enough to fully decapitate the stranger. Jack pulled the blade free and finished the job with one more swing of the cleaver.

The man's head tumbled off his shoulders.

And he caught it in his outstretched hands.

Staring up at him, the head said, "You have some serious anger management issues, Jack."

Jack screamed and ran out of the room.

He raced into the bedroom he'd shared with Lorene for so many months and barricaded the door by pushing the dresser in front of it. Then he stepped back and stood staring at the blocked door while he huffed and puffed. Then he cursed himself for continuing to behave like a fucking moron. He'd made the mistake of every bubble-headed bimbo in every dimwitted slasher movie ever made. He'd trapped himself in another room inside his home instead of *fleeing* the goddamn place.

Jack seized handfuls of his hair and shrieked.

"Severed...heads...don't...TALK!"

Of course they didn't. And Jack dismissed the notion that he'd actually seen this happen. This was just added confirmation that he'd suffered a psychotic break. Something in him had snapped when confronted with the visual evidence of Lorene's infidelity, a crucial component of his soul that was just irreparably broken.

I need to kill myself, he thought.

I can't live like this.

He heard a sigh behind him. "Jack, if you kill yourself, you'll burn in the lake of fire. And you don't want that, trust me. But them's the rules, buddy."

Jack remained where he was.

Why bother confronting a stubborn hallucination?

"You're...not...there. You...don't...exist."

"Jack, look at me."

There was some steel in the intruder's voice now. The jovial quality was gone. Jack felt helplessly compelled to obey it.

He swallowed hard and turned around.

The stranger was sitting on the edge of the bed. He was still cradling his head in his hands. The stern expression on his face sent a shudder through Jack. It should have been an absurd tableau: a still-sentient decapitated head and a still-mobile headless body.

But Jack didn't feel like laughing.

He cast his memory backward several moments. He saw the cleaver blade entering the stranger's neck again. Then a second time. And he remembered the lack of spurting blood. There'd been no blood at all.

Jack cleared his throat and said, "What are you?"

The stern expression melted, giving way to a grin. The hands lifted the head to its former spot between the body's shoulders, set it down, and wrenched it into place. There was a bit of grunting and the stranger grimaced. The hands came away from the head and the head stayed in place.

It looked to have been seamlessly restored, the skin perfect and unbroken.

The stranger made a sound of relief. "Aaaaah! Much better."

Jack swallowed another lump in his throat.

He was starting to feel sick again.

The stranger rubbed his hands together briskly, then clapped them once, like a door to door salesman about to make a pitch. "So, Jack, you wanted some personal info?"

Feeling like Alice falling through the hole, Jack nodded once.

The stranger grinned. "Jack, I'm your guardian angel."

Jack grunted. "Really."

"Yep." The grin gave way to a more solemn expression. "Look, I understand that you're skeptical. Guardian angels don't show up every day, otherwise you'd hear about it, right? We're just in old movies, right? Wrong. Thing is, not everybody has a guardian angel. It's sort of a spiritual reward, Jack. You get one assigned to watch over your soul if you've done something truly extraordinary in a past life."

Jack frowned. "Yeah? So what did I do to make me special?"

The angel smiled and shook his head. "I can't tell you much, Jack. It's just not allowed. You did a great thing in a past life, a truly extraordinary, selfless act of rare heroism. And you died in the process."

Jack liked the sound of that. Thinking of himself as a hero rather than a maniacal murderer was infinitely more pleasing to the soul. "I was in a war, huh?"

Saying it out loud, Jack knew it was true.

No hidden memory from his former life emerged through the fog of the past, but he felt the truth of the statement in his bones. It was an immutable fact. Somewhere on the other side of the earth, and in another body, he'd died on a battlefield.

A noble, honorable death.

Tears welled in his eyes.

The angel shrugged. "I can neither confirm nor deny that, Jackie boy. I can't tell you anything other than what I've already said. On that subject, that is. I'm here to make you an offer, my friend."

He started walking toward Jack.

Jack's knees began to shake.

The angel placed his hands on Jack's shoulders and gazed at him with sympathetic eyes. "Jack, I'm gonna offer what amounts to a heavenly get out of jail free card. You have a choice. You can do as you wished. You can reverse what's happened. You can undo it. Or..." He glanced away a moment, appearing to hesitate. His gaze came back to Jack. "Or you can say no and face God's judgment now."

Jack swallowed a lump. "What, and go to hell?"

The angel shrugged. "That's not for me to say, Jack. You can ask God for forgiveness, but it's up to Him whether He grants it. And I can't tell you what he'd do, because I honestly don't know."

Jack grunted. "So my choice is obvious."

The angel cocked an eyebrow. "Is it?"

Jack laughed. "Isn't it? I can put things right. Lorene and that coffee shop asshole can live again." A tentative smile tugged at the corners of his mouth as he thought about the possibilities. "And I can atone by living a better life, an exemplary life. I'll do good deeds and do what I can to make the world a better place."

The angel's eyes crinkled and he sniffled. "That's beautiful, man."

Gentle mockery.

Jack rolled his eyes. "I'm serious."

Some of the humor faded from the angel's eyes. "I know you are, Jack. And I respect you for it. So I'm going to do this thing for you. I hope you make the best of your second chance, my friend. Be forewarned, however—you'll be cursed with the memory of what you did. Undoing the deed will not free your conscience of this burden. It will haunt you." He sighed. "I'll leave you with a piece of advice—keep your head down and your powder dry."

Jack frowned.

The words seemed familiar and resonant, like some dimly recalled bit of dialogue from a long-ago movie. For a moment, he was transported beyond this time and place, and his senses were clogged with an omnipresent stench of death and the sputtering cough of machine gun fire.

The memory snap passed in a nanosecond.

Like a firefly darting in and out of his field of vision.

The angel stepped back. He smiled. "Let's do this, man. Kinda in a hurry here, pard. There's a Salvation Ale with my name on it, and I'm feelin' mighty thirsty."

He clapped his hands.

Said something in a language Jack didn't recognize.

And disappeared.

Jack blinked.

He experienced a jarring sense of displacement. He was standing at the door to his apartment. He had his overnight bag slung over his shoulder and the key to his apartment in his right hand.

He hesitated.

He placed an ear to the door and listened.

He heard heavy breathing.

Lorene moaning.

So it was true. Not that he hadn't been presented with enough incontrovertible evidence already. Still, it was disconcerting to find his desperate wish granted. Lorene was alive on the other side of this door, getting passionate with the coffee shop stud.

Jack experienced a brief surge of his former anger.

He suppressed it.

He keyed open the door, drew in a calming breath, and stepped inside to confront the unpleasantness awaiting him. The shirtless stud reacted as before, yelping and grabbing his shirt. Jack clenched his fists tight as the mumbling, blushing kid stumbled by him.

The fists remained at his sides.

Jack released the breath he'd been holding and went to the sofa, where he sat down next to Lorene. Lorene didn't say anything. She picked up her blouse, shrugged it on, and calmly started to button it.

Jack said, "I forgive you, Lorene."

And then she began to cry.

He took her in his arms and held her.

After several months of soul-searching and many counseling sessions, Jack and Lorene got married. Jack impressed her by becoming a more sensitive man and a better, more attentive lover. He did the good deeds he'd promised the angel, donating significant portions of each paycheck to a variety of worthy causes.

All was well in Jack's world.

Well, not quite all.

He did have nightmares about what he'd done prior to being granted his second chance. Mostly he didn't remember them, but there'd been one so lucid it had almost seemed real. In this dream, he went further than he had in reality. In the dream, his state of intense arousal was not to be denied.

In the dream, he did...things...unspeakable, awful, sick *things* to Lorene's limbless, headless torso.

Jack awoke from the dream feeling ill, barely making it to the bathroom in time to vomit his steak dinner into the toilet bowl.

Thankfully, that dream had not recurred.

And his waking life was filled with joy.

Then one night he went out for a walk. He stopped at a street corner to dig change out of his pocket for a newspaper. While he was counting out his change, a compact car with tinted windows rolled up beside him.

The passenger side window rolled down.

A vaguely familiar voice called out to him: "Mr. Roth!"

Frowning, Jack turned around.

For the slightest fraction of a moment, he perceived the muzzle flash of a pistol. Then he gasped as the first of three slugs slammed into his chest.

He fell dead to the sidewalk and the car peeled off.

Lorene snatched up the phone on the first ring.

A shivery sensation of pleasure snaked through her as she heard the beloved voice: "We're free, baby."

Lorene squeaked with delight. "Yes! You did it? You really did it?"

Jeb Marshall laughed. "Of course. You know I'd do anything for you. You should be hearing from the police soon."

Lorene gasped. "Oooh! Let's not talk about it over the phone."

Jeb laughed again. "Gotcha. Listen, when it's all over, we'll celebrate our freedom at Mondo Java. Meanwhile, I hope you're prepared to face the music."

Lorene smiled and twisted the phone cord in her hands, wishing it was Jeb's hair. "Don't worry about me, I'll be fine."

"Coolness. Better go now. Hang in there, babe. I love you."

"Love you, too."

Lorene returned the phone to its cradle.

The prospect of facing the police made her a little nervous, but that wasn't enough to dampen her excitement; she was beside herself with unalloyed joy. She was so glad she'd gone through these months of agony. All those stupid counseling sessions with Jack had been so worth it. Christ, to think they'd almost blown it when Jack came back from the airport that time.

It was a good life lesson.

When you get another chance to do things right, grab the fucker.

Lorene poured herself a cup of French roast, sipped from the steaming mug, and began practicing grief-stricken widow faces.

JARHEAD

My best friend growing up was this guy named Mark Angel. Mark flaked out in college, ran away with the circus, and eventually dropped off the radar screen. I got postcards from him for a while, mostly from points south. The postmarks were from backwater burgs in Florida, Alabama, Louisiana, and Texas. The postcards arrived intermittently over a period of several months, then they just stopped coming. That was fourteen years ago.

Mark was just a memory—a long-forgotten one.

Until Resurrection Week, that is.

Check this out.

Saturday morning. The alarm was trilling inches away from my ear. I reached for the snooze button, then it dawned on me the sound I was hearing wasn't the alarm—it was the telephone. I rolled onto my side, blinked away the last vestiges of sleep, and stared at the blatting monstrosity.

Then I looked at the clock.

"Aw, shit."

The time was 9:07 a.m., too early by far for a sleep-in Saturday.

But the insolent device kept on ringing. Fucker.

"Jesus Christ, Craig, pick up the goddamn phone." A pillow thumped the back of my head. "Or I'll be forced to wrap the cord around your neck."

The assailant was Jenny Hollis. Her presence there was a sign that a sort of sea change was underway in my life. Jenny was no dubious barroom conquest. I'd known her nearly half my life. She was the second girl who ever consented to have sex with me, when I was barely nineteen. We were together intermittently over the next several years. We experienced periods of great passion, and I suppose she should have been the great love of my life. It just didn't happen.

Now, however, we were together yet again. Reconciliation No. 123,000, give or take.

I picked up the phone. "Yeah?"

"Is this Craig McTavish?"

My first thought was, Bill Collector.

"Ah..."

Remember, I hadn't heard Mark's voice in over a decade. The caller paused a moment before speaking again. "Um... McT?"

I almost dropped the phone. "Mark?"

No one else would call me "McT."

Mark chuckled. "McT. I knew it was you, man."

I glanced at Jenny. "I'm think I'm talking to Mark Angel."

"Only I'm the one doing all the talking," I heard Mark say.

Jenny's eyes widened. "Mark Angel is alive?"

"Evidently."

Mark said, "I'm alive and well, old friend—though I understand your skepticism. I've been gone a long time."

I grunted. "Huh. Yeah. A long time. Where the hell have you been, Mark?"

He sighed. "You're angry, sure. I've been on a long journey. You gotta believe me when I say I never meant to be gone so long."

A long journey?

What do you say to an understatement of such epic proportions?

Mark kept talking. "We've got to hook up. There's so much I need to tell you, things I wouldn't feel comfortable talking about over the phone."

Things like Jarhead—but I didn't know that at the time.

I ultimately agreed to meet with Mark just to get him off the phone. I returned the receiver to its cradle, went to Jenny, and we made love with a fervor I'd never felt with anyone else.

Later, when we sat down to a late breakfast, Jenny began her interrogation. Naturally, she wanted to know everything about my conversation with Mark. There wasn't much to tell, but she perked up when I said I'd arranged to meet with Mark.

"Oh! You have to take me!"

I shrugged. "Sure. Why not?"

I had agreed to meet Mark at a nearby state park at around three that afternoon. By the time we hit the road, I was close to eager to see my old friend. We stopped at a convenience store for a twelve-pack of Corona, a Styrofoam cooler, and a bag of ice.

We talked about Mark during the drive to the park. A familiar portrait emerged from our shared memories, that of a reckless young man who liked to put himself in harm's way. He was self-destructive, but he sought his ruin in such colorful and interesting ways we didn't think of it as self-destructiveness.

Ah, the beautiful stupidity of youth.

We pulled into the park entrance at 2:45. We drove more than a mile down a winding two-lane road, then, as we came around yet another bend, a sparsely populated parking lot came into view. The only other vehicle present was an old, weather-beaten VW van. I reached into the cooler for a long-necked bottle of Corona as Jenny guided my old Camaro into a parking space.

Jenny smirked. "So where's Lazarus?"

"The lake. He said he'd be fishing off a pier."

Beyond the parking lot was a narrow footpath that wound down a hill. I followed Jenny down the path, watching her ass move in the white shorts. She was wearing a skimpy yellow bikini top, and I knew there was a matching bottom beneath the shorts. The shorts were low-slung and hugged her hips. Her long legs were toned and brown from the sun. She was wearing sunglasses and her blonde hair was pulled back in a scrunchy. She looked like a model in a tanning lotion ad.

I'm trying to communicate a sense of lust here, okay?

I've never desired a woman more than I desired Jenny.

The ground leveled out as we stepped through a stand of

trees and emerged again into the bright light of the sun. We saw picnic tables and plastic-lined trash cans. About twenty yards beyond the picnic area, a short pier extended over the water. I squinted and was able to make out a solitary figure at the end of the pier, a shirtless man with long, curly hair casting a line into the water.

Jenny came to a stop, and I pulled up right beside her.

I swallowed hard. "It's him."

Jenny's reply was a nervous whisper. "Yes."

"Let's do this."

Jenny just nodded.

I saw Mark set down his rod and reel and pick up a can of Heineken. He leaned against the railing and watched our approach behind inscrutable black sunglasses.

His voice boomed out to us. "McT! And is that the ever-lovely Jenny Hollis I see by your side?"

Jenny was unable to suppress the smile that came to her lips. Mark had always been a charmer. "Hi, Mark."

Mark was remarkably fit for a man his age, with an abundance of toned muscles and barely a hint of flab anywhere on his body. But he wasn't a dead-ringer for the twenty-year-old I remembered. There was a weathered quality to his face. He looked like a man who had spent the bulk of his life getting baked by the sun.

Mark extended a hand. "Good to see you again, bro."

I shook his hand. "Yeah."

Mark drained the rest of his Heineken. "Let's snag us a picnic table and commence to reminiscing."

Mark picked up his rod and reel, propped it over his shoulder, and began to make his way down the pier. We were right behind him. We parked ourselves at the nearest table, and I fished more beers out of the cooler.

Mark popped open another Heineken. "So," he said, "who wants to go first?"

We sat there in silence for a while. We were a conglomeration of nervous smiles and fidgety hands. I looked at Mark. I looked at Jenny. I drank some beer. And I said, "That's a no-brainer, pal. You're the one who buggered off when Ronnie Raygun was still prez."

Mark set the Heineken can down. He sighed. "My parents did some fucked-up shit to me when I was a kid. The most perverse, ugly shit you could imagine."

I frowned. "Jesus."

"It stopped soon after I entered high school." He smiled crookedly. "I was suddenly old enough and big enough to fight back, so they left me alone. Then when we got to college I started doing every drug known to man in mass quantities." He smiled ruefully. "Kinda hard to keep up with your studies when you're watching miniature marching bands prance across your dorm room floor."

Jenny laughed. "I can see how that would pose a distraction."

Mark smiled at her. "Yeah, but I was able to hang on for a while. Then the circus came to town. Well, a traveling carnival. I met some of the carnies in a bar one night. They seemed like cool guys." He smirked. "They talked a lot about drugs. And they made life on the road seem like the most romantic adventurous way of life imaginable." He shrugged. "So I joined up."

I shook my head. "And bailed out of your life—not to mention the lives of your friends."

Mark sighed. "Don't think I didn't feel bad about that, Craig. Hell, I was only with the carnies for a few months. They were too wild even for me. I took off on my own. I didn't come back for the same reason I never told anybody the truth about my parents—I just couldn't deal. I couldn't explain myself. So I stayed away."

I finished another Corona. "If you were only with them a few months..."

Mark went on to describe a nomadic life. He spent a significant portion of those lost years following hippie jam bands around. He enjoyed the tribal lifestyle of the traveling hippies, and he eked out a living by selling them drugs.

I felt no inclination to hide my exasperation. "Why are you back here, man? You tired of being a highway gypsy? Are you back to stay?"

Mark frowned.

I arched an eyebrow. "Well?"

He managed a weak smile. "I can see the pity in your eyes, McT. You think I've wasted my life."

Bull's eye.

"I only think you've squandered a great deal of potential. You're smart, Mark, smarter than just about anybody I've ever known. You could've been anything you wanted to be."

His smile broadened a little. "But, Craig, I am what I want to be. I never dreamed of running a corporation, or whatever it is you think I should have devoted my life to. I've got a freedom I never would've had if I'd gone that way."

I sighed. "Okay."

There was a dismissive tone to my voice.

Neither of them missed it. Jenny, who'd been stewing quietly while Mark and I bantered, shot me a scornful glare.

"You should listen to him, Mark, he's the expert on squandered potential." She abruptly got up and stalked away. "I'm going for a walk," she called over her shoulder. "Do me a favor and don't come after me."

I met Mark's gaze. I tried to read his expression, but there was nothing there—no evidence of concern or embarrassment. A friend will usually make a token show of concern under such circumstances, but Mark looked like a man with no worries.

I grunted. "She'll be okay. We're just having a little tiff."

Mark grinned. "You bet."

I wondered how long it had been since Mark had related to other people in any real, human way. His general oddness made me uncomfortable, and I didn't want to be around him a moment longer than necessary. I tried to send a mental message to Jenny. I throw myself on your mercy, babe—I'm a shit, you have every reason to be disappointed in me, let's call it a day and get the hell out of here.

She was still walking along the shoreline. I considered disregarding her request to leave her alone. Hell, she probably wanted me to come after her, regardless of what she said.

I looked at Mark. "I hate to say this, man, but—"

He held up a hand to shush me. "Whoa, hold on. I know you

want to hit the road, but there's something in my van I want to show you before we say goodbye."

I sighed.

"Come on, McT, you might never see me again." His eyes glimmered with sudden tears. "Just indulge me for a few minutes, okay?"

Well, what harm could it do?

I stood up, cupped my hands around my mouth, and called out to Jenny. "Hey, Jen! Mark's got something he wants to show me in his van. We'll just be a few minutes, okay?"

She turned toward us, smiled, and waved.

That reassuring smile warmed my heart. I felt emboldened enough to add, "I love you, Jen!"

Her reply made me happier than I'd been in, oh, forever: "I love you, too!"

Just like that, all the tension drained from my body.

I grinned at Mark. "She loves me."

He said, "I know."

So I followed him back up the path to the parking lot. When we reached the van, Mark gripped a rusty door handle and drew the sliding door partway open.

He ushered me in with a sweep of his hand. "After you, sir."

I stepped up into the murky semi-darkness of the van. The grimy windows diffused the light of the sun. I took a seat on a bench toward the rear of the van and surveyed the vehicle's seedy interior. It was evident to me that the van was Mark's real home. There were crates of books and cassette tapes. A rolled-up sleeping bag sat atop one of them.

Mark took a seat opposite me on another bench. The bench was right behind the van's front seats. Mark peeked through the gap between the seats, then returned his attention to me.

"Welcome to my humble abode."

I cast a phony appraising glance around. "Yeah. Um...how old is this ride, Mark?"

"It's a '71. I've had it since my carnie days. I liberated it from a dude I worked with, a carnie." He flashed a disturbing, almost demented grin flashed again. "He didn't need it anymore, anyway."

Shit. The guy seemed different now...stranger.

I cleared my throat. “Yeah...didn’t you have something to show me?”

“Oh, yeah, sorry.” He glanced again through the gap between the front seats. “The dude I got the van from, I got something else from him, too.”

He turned and reached between the seats. He lifted something off the passenger seat, then gingerly brought it through the gap between the seats.

It was a container of some kind. Mark set the container down on the bench, got up, and duck walked to my end of the van. He had a flashlight in his hand, though I couldn’t recall seeing him retrieve it.

“Let’s shed some light on the situation.”

He flicked on the flashlight, directed its beam at the container, and I felt a hot lump of fear rise into my throat. My chest felt tight. I thought I might be having a heart attack. Not that it mattered, since I was obviously in the presence of a psychopath. No way would he allow me to live after seeing this.

The container was a large glass jar with a metal lid. It was filled with formaldehyde. Floating inside was a severed human head.

Mark said, “That’s Jarhead.”

The head looked like it’d belonged to a middle-aged Caucasian male. Its eyes were wide and staring, and its longish silver hair floated in the solution like strands of seaweed.

“Jarhead, say hello to my friend Craig.”

I looked at him. “Why?”

Mark frowned. “Why what?”

“Why did you kill him?”

Mark smiled. “I didn’t kill the guy, Craig. You should listen better. I got Jarhead from the guy who used to have this van.”

“And what happened to that guy?”

“Oh, him I killed.”

“Oh.”

“The guy needed killing. He ripped me off. I don’t know if he killed our encapsulated friend.” He nodded at Jarhead. “But I don’t think so. Jarhead’s been around a long time. He told me once he was a research scientist in the 50's."

"Who told you that?"

"Jarhead."

I nodded. Uh-huh. You're a psycho, Mark. "You and Jarhead talk a lot?"

"I know you think I'm crazy, Craig. Sane people don't tend to have an ongoing dialogue with severed heads. But it's the truth. I hear his voice inside my head." He tapped his skull. "He's smart. You wanted to know how I've supported myself all these years. Well, dealing drugs is part of it, but I generate the bulk of my income by following Jarhead's suggestions."

"Uh-huh."

"You could say he's my guiding spirit. My sensei. My Jedi master." He wasn't smiling anymore. "He's the reason I'm back here, Craig."

"Jarhead said you should come home?"

Mark nodded. "He said I needed to see you."

"Yeah?"

Mark sighed. "Don't think this isn't hard for me, Craig. But I have to do what I have to do." He clamped a strong hand around my throat. "Jarhead says I need to exorcise the demons of my past. He says I'll only be happy if I can stop thinking about what I left behind."

His grip around my throat tightened.

I gurgled.

Tears streamed from the corners of his eyes. "I'll go see my parents tonight. They're more deserving of this than you, man, but I've got no choice. You've got to see that, buddy."

I tried to pry his hand away, but he was too strong. I couldn't breathe. I began to feel lightheaded. His eyes bulged from the strain of strangling me. The moment I stopped struggling was when I heard her voice.

"Craig? Mark?" It was Jenny; she was standing just outside the van. "What are you guys doing in there?"

Mark's head whipped toward the door. "Fuck!"

"Craig?"

Mark's hands came away from my throat. I sucked in a ragged gasp of air and tried to find my voice, but it was no use.

I desperately wanted to warn her, but all I could manage was a helpless wheeze.

Then Mark was moving toward the door. I tumbled to the floor and extended a weak hand toward him—it brushed limply against his ankle before thumping on the floor. I saw him haul the door open, reach outside, and drag Jenny inside.

Mark killed her.

I don't wish to describe her death in any detail. He didn't do anything especially cruel. It was over in a heartbeat. But a part of me died in that moment, too. The most important part, I suspect.

It was while Mark was staring at her broken body that I recovered a measure of strength. Adrenaline likely played a role in what happened next. I picked up my discarded Corona bottle, surged to my feet, and broke the bottle over Mark's head. He toppled backward, crashing through the gap between the front seats.

I loomed over him with a broken shard of bottle in my hand. He tried to push himself up. But I planted a knee on his chest, drove him back down, and sliced open his throat with the jagged wedge of glass. There was a lot of blood. But not enough. There could never be enough to avenge Jenny.

I dropped the shard of glass and got out of the van. I couldn't look at Jenny's corpse. I might've killed myself if I'd looked at her then. I collapsed against the van, slid down until I was sitting on the ground, where I stayed for a long time.

I stayed there until a park ranger came around.

The ranger had a look inside the van. A long look. Then he told me, "Stay there. I'm getting the cops."

I nodded.

But I didn't stay right there. I did something while the ranger was in his car. I removed something from the van. I was sure I was losing my mind—there could be no sane reason for what I was doing—but I felt compelled to do it.

The cops showed up. Lots of them. Turns out Mark had left a trail of bodies all over the country, as well as a substantial trail of circumstantial and physical evidence. The FBI would have taken him down eventually.

Which wasn't exactly a comfort.

Several weeks have passed.

My world is in a shambles.

My hope for the future is gone. Too late, I've realized how completely that hope centered on Jenny. My guilt is beyond quantifying.

The guilt isn't the worst thing, though.

Jarhead is the worst thing. Lately I've begun to hear his voice in my head.

I bought a gun with the last of my money. A Desert Eagle. The handgun equivalent of a cannon. I'm hoping I somehow become brave enough to put its barrel in my mouth.

Because, God help me, I think Jarhead has something else in mind.

This recording is for the benefit of anyone I might hurt at his behest.

Please know this.

Whatever I've done, Jarhead made me do it.

I love you, Jenny.

Forgive me.

SUSTENANCE

Kent Hogan eased his Toyota Camry to a stop as the light turned red. The bright crimson orb glared at him like the eye of a demon, a luminescent puncture wound in the black flesh of night. He averted his gaze, but he could feel the heat of the eye upon him, probing his brains like a surgical laser.

Brian surgery, now there was an idea worth exploring.

Some extensive frontal lobe work, perhaps, to excise the malignant knot of melancholy that had taken root there and grown beyond his ability to combat.

The city street appeared deserted, which wasn't surprising at this hour. The bars had closed an hour earlier, disgorging the usual array of DUI candidates. By now, the drunks were all either home, in jail, or splattered in a mess of managed metal on the highway.

The buildings to his left and right were all dark. No cars passed through the crossing street. Kent wondered why the traffic lights here didn't flash that intermittent yellowpulse the way they did in other cities in the empty hours.

He sighed.

And thought, *because I'm in Bumfuck, Nowhere, the asshole of the universe.*

Kent had been stricken with a terminal case of wanderlust in the waning days of his joyless marriage to Amy. One day, a bright, cloudless day in late August, he'd been washing the Camry in the driveway of their well-tended suburban home. He remembered twisting a sponge thick with soap and grit over a mop bucket, watching the stream of dirty water splash into the bucket. He remembered looking up and taking note of the way the sun glinted off the windshield of the Camry, making it sparkle in a way that caused his heart to ache with inchoate desire he couldn't quite articulate.

He dropped the sponge in the bucket, sprayed the soap off the car with hose, and drove away from his home.

Away from Amy.

He hadn't seen her since.

The notion of returning to Amy to be forgiveness for his flight occasionally flitted through his mind, but he knew he would never submit himself to that humiliation.

Anyway, what could he tell her about why he'd left?

He remained unsure of the actual reasons himself.

His gaze went back to the traffic light.

Still red.

And it had been red an awfully long time.

Why on earth would this light not change?

He sighed.

And thought, *so just go through it*.

Hell, there was no one around.

No pedestrians.

No patrol cars.

Nothing.

Still, he hesitated. He checked his rearview mirror, saw nothing there, and again scanned the road ahead of him.

He was utterly fucking alone in the dead of this cold night in this strange city.

He longed for home.

Tears stung his eyes.

Home?

What a fucking joke. He didn't have one anymore.

Kent blew out a breath. "Jesus Christ…I'm having a nervous breakdown."

Get yourself back to the hotel, he thought.

It just wouldn't do to suffer the long-delayed total mental meltdown he knew was coming while stuck at a malfunctioning traffic light. He was alone for the moment, yes, but that was subject to change as long as he remained here.

His foot began to ease off the brake pedal.

And that was when he saw her—long, skinny legs encased in ripped fishnets at the edge of his field of vision. His eyes tracked her as she crossed the intersection, taking note of her unsteady gait on those ridiculously high red stiletto heels. She glanced his way as she passed the car, and he shuddered at the sight of eyes so hollow they hinted at a soul emptier and more damaged than his own. Dark eyes that were a startling contrast to flesh so sickly pale Kent knew she was a drug addict. Her expression revealed nothing, a slack, flat mask of numb indifference.

She reached the other side of the street, stumbled once as a heel skidded over the curb, and looked both ways before continuing across the crossing street. She reached the other side and continued down the sidewalk.

Kent looked up.

The light was green.

He tapped the accelerator and the Camry rolled through the intersection. But his foot slid back to the brake pedal, and he exerted enough pressure to keep the car inching along behind the girl.

He kept expecting her to look back and notice him, but she just continued down the sidewalk, her head down, her long, permed blonde hair hanging in her face. She wore a microshirt that clung to her skinny ass like shrink wrap. A battered leather jacket covered the sheer, flesh-exposing top he'd glimpsed when she passed him.

Kent became aware of moisture at the corners of his mouth.

This was all very alarming.

What am I doing? he wondered.

He supposed she was a strung-out prostitute. He thought about the wad of cash in his wallet, which had dipped below two-hundred dollars. It was all he had left, and he couldn't afford to blow any of it on a hooker.

She looked weak, used-up, just another of society's wasted cast-offs.

How hard could it be to pull her into the car and subdue her?

Then…

Kent was repulsed by the sick turn of his thoughts. There was a lot wrong with him, obviously; he was depressed, borderline suicidal, and he was a day or two away from facing some pretty hard choices, decisions that would either pull him out his this self-destructive spiral or speed him down the path toward absolute ruin. Pretty hardcore stuff. But he wasn't a bad man. He'd never entertained—even for the briefest moment—thoughts as evil and perverse as these.

He'd hit the road in search of…something. He didn't know what, but something. Something new. Something revelatory. Something inspiring. Something beautiful. Some nugget of perfect truth he could seize hold of and use as a way of replenishing the missing parts of his soul.

The object of his search, whatever it really was, remained elusive, but he knew one thing: he hadn't begun this strange journey to embark on a career as a serial killer.

He decided he should drive on past the pitiful whore.

But his foot didn't come off the brake pedal.

His grip tightened around the steering wheel.

His breath wheezed in and out through clenched teeth.

The girl's gait remained unsteady as she continued down the sidewalk, but she walked in a more-or-less straight line. Kent felt pity for her. He knew the kind of concentration it required to walk like that when you were that high, an intensity of focus that blotted out everything else. He saw that she was on a collision course with a glass-enclosed bus stop, and it was fascinating to watch, like seeing a slow-motion replay of a car crash. She just kept stumbling along until her forehead smacked the glass.

She wobbled on her heels. One foot came off the ground, and her arms pinwheeled in a desperate effort to regain balance.

To no avail.

She pitched backward, landing hard on her ass and crying out.

Kent pulled the Camry to the curb and got out. He went to the girl and knelt beside her, his nervous hands fluttering around her, wanting to touch, to calm, to…touch.

He sucked moisture from the corners of his mouth again.

"Miss, are you okay? Can I help you?"

Her eyes screwed shut, but they fluttered open now.

Kent's hands settled around her waist, and he was momentarily unable to breath. She felt insubstantial, ephemeral, light as a pillow. He was aware of his car behind him of how very close it was.

He could have her inside it in an instant.

He could have her.

His gaze slid away from her face, traced the length of her long legs, lingering on the patches of pale flesh exposed by rips in the fishnets. He could feel his soul growing cold, his essence, his identity as a decent man, disappearing down a very dark hole, like blood swirling down a shower drain.

And he knew he was going to do it.

Sentence himself to an eternity in hell.

Despite the clamor of admonishing voices in his head—the nattering voices of ingrained lessons about right and wrong, good and bad—he was going to do it. He would deal with the damage to his conscience later.

Anyway, maybe this really was the object of this strange journey.

A long-sought opportunity to release the darkness within him.

His grip tightened about the girl's waist.

He gasped as she seized handfuls of his shirt, twisting the shirt with strength such a wasted wretch couldn't possibly possess. She pulled him close, and her eyes glittered like black diamonds, unclouded by drugs and full of need.

Full of hunger.

Her formerly slack features bloomed with life and color, her mouth stretching thin in a wide, ghastly grin, exposing rows of jagged teeth. He saw something yellow and worm-like fluttering at the back of her mouth. She pulled him closer, wrapping her stockinged legs tight around him on the sidewalk.

Kent struggled, but it was no use; her legs trapped him as efficiently as a block of wood in a vise. His heart thudded and he felt the sharp bite of acid reflux at the back of his throat. He'd only been this frightened one other time in his life, when he was a little boy and the older boys across the street did the awful things to him, the things his memory had shielded him from until now.

Kent chocked out a phlegm sob.

He was facing probably death at the hands of some inexplicable creature that was merely masquerading as a human woman, but that didn't matter; he truly didn't care that he was facing death. Because he suddenly knew what was wrong with him, knew where all the pain came from, irreparable damage no doctor could ever expunge.

The girl-thing pulled him closer.

Her face distended, became an elastic mask that mocked her former prettiness. Her mouth was a wide oval, and the yellow thing inside it grew larger, pulsing like an aroused cock. Then it surged forward, pushed through his own open mouth, and the creature began to feed, drawing sustenance from his suffering.

His mind played a fast-forward catalogue of all the painful events from his life, thirty years worth of regrets and heartbreak. The early heart attack death of his father, the suicide of his alcoholic sister, the loss of his one true love (not Amy), his unfulfilled dreams, getting married to Amy because she was pregnant, the subsequent miscarriage, and the nightmares he never remembered upon awakening, surreal dream-world distortions of what the older boys did to him in that basement.

All of it.

Every disappointment.

Every fractured hope.

Each of them like a little death.

Ending with his conflicted thoughts on the sidewalk a few moments ago.

Then he felt the yellow thing—the probe, the feeder tube—retract, and he sucked in air, the automatic, involuntary act of a still-living organism. The creature's legs loosened around him by slow degrees, and he saw her face reorganize itself, a strange, pliable putty that again formed a startling facsimile of an attractive woman's face.

It was smiling.

A glowing visage that radiated satiation.

Which was the opposite of the way Kent felt. He was a husk, a hollowed-out shell of his former self. He barely had enough energy to breathe. The girl-thing gave him a shove, and he tumbled away from her.

He was on his back on the sidewalk.

Staring up at the stars in the sky.

The infinite expanse of space spoke to him, whispering of an ascent to a celestial abyss, a place where there was no hurt, just eternal nothingness, pure, perfect absence of all things composing the human condition.

His vision blurred.

The twinkling points of light above him became white blotches, sloppy smears on a faded canvas.

He dimly perceived a sound of stiletto heels clicking down the sidewalk, moving way from him.

Then the world was gone.

Amy Hogan put aside the Maeve Binchy novel she'd been reading when she heard the front door creak open. Her pulse quickened, and a paralyzing rush of fear pinned her to the living room recliner.

The closest phone was in the kitchen. She knew she could get to it and punch in 9-1-1 before the intruder had a chance to get to her. She glanced that way, swallowed hard, and remained where she was.

She heard footsteps in the foyer.

Followed by the sound of the door being pushed gently shut.

Then a rattle of keys.

No, she thought.

It can't be him.

In the early days following Kent's unexplained departure, she'd been surrounded by friends seeking to comfort her, people who told her she'd be all right eventually, that the passage of time would heal her emotional wounds. What she'd been unable to tell them—the thing she wouldn't voice to even her closest girlfriends—was the sad truth of the situation; that she wasn't heartbroken over her husband's abandonment of her.

What she mostly felt was relief.

And she'd felt gratitude when her friends thought she should feel only anger. None of them knew the real truth of her marriage to Kent, that it had been a loveless sham from the beginning, a case of two broken people brought together by circumstance.

The footsteps grew louder.

Then Kent stepped through the archway into the living room.

Amy's heart sank.

Go away, she thought.

Go away and never come back.

She sigh. "You're back."

Kent shrugged. "Yeah."

He sounded tired.

He looked worse, emaciated, like a heroin chic model from the early 90's, only in Kent's case there was no accompanying hint of decadent glamour. He wore ill-fitting clothes, a billowy t-shirt and baggy jeans that accentuated his gaunt appearance, made him look like a stickman.

Amy felt a twinge of sympathy. "Kent…what the fuck?"

She couldn't think of anything else to say—the situation was beyond inexplicable. Her husband had been gone nearly two months, and now he'd returned looking like an Auschwitz survivor. She knew he'd withdrawn a couple grand from the bank the day of his disappearance, which wasn't a fortune, but it meant there was no good reason he should be looking this bad.

So "What the fuck?" was pretty much the prefect summation of her feelings.

Kent opened his mouth to say something, but the words died on the tip of his tongue.

His lower lip trembled.

And then he was crying, his misty eyes yielding fat tears that rolled quickly down his cheeks, a waterfall of inarticulate emotion.

Amy sighed again.

She got to her feet and went to him, pulling him into a half-hearted embrace. She patted his back and made cooing noises. "There, there, baby, it's okay. You just get it all out, cry until you're dry, then we'll talk about it, okay?"

She lifted her head off his shoulder and smiled at him.

Then he was smiling, too.

Amy stepped back.

He seized her wrists, halting her sudden backward motion.

And his smile kept expanding, growing exponentially more obscene by the moment.

She opened her mouth to scream.

He smothered the scream with his own mouth.

Then she felt something warm enter her, something thick, slimy, and pulsating, and she was pretty sure it was that awful yellow thing she'd glimpsed at the back of his throat.

But then she wasn't thinking about that anymore.

She was a kid again, watching her daddy hit her mommy.

She was a teenage virgin, an innocent being assaulted by a predator the police were never able to apprehend.

And she was an unhappy mother-to-be who felt only shameful relief when she miscarried.

And more, so much more.

A parade of misery.

The, worst of all, she was left alive on the living room floor.

With something new growing inside of her.

KILLERS ON THE ROAD

The old Chevelle was parked in a corner of the convenience store's parking lot, its front end pointed toward the street. An Escalade with fake bullet hole stickers on the driver's side door rolled to a slow stop at the nearby intersection. Heather Campbell tracked the Escalade's snail-like progress through squinted eyes, an ugly scowl painted on otherwise lovely—albeit haggard—features.

"Why do people do that?"

Josh Browning, slumped down in the shotgun seat, blinked at her through eyes bleary from smoking too much weed. "Huh?" He sat up straighter, and his head swiveled slowly to the right. He squinted at the Escalade, which was now sliding through the intersection on its way, no doubt, to some appropriately white trash destination. Then his head wobbled back in her direction. "Why do people drive Escalades? All sorts of reasons, I guess. It's an individual thing. It all depends on what you want out of a car and—"

Heather heaved an exasperated sigh. "Why do people put fake bullet hole decals on their fucking cars, man? Would it kill you to stop blazing up for a just a few minutes and pay some goddamn attention to what I'm saying?"

Josh glanced at the crumpled joint hanging pinched loosely between his thumb and forefinger. He shrugged and stubbed the lit end out in the Chevelle's overflowing ashtray. "Sorry. I guess people do that because they think it makes them look badass."

Heather's scowl deepened. "It makes them look like fucking idiots."

"Yeah."

"If you were a real criminal, like of the violent, dangerous variety, why would you tool around in a shot-up ride?" Josh opened his mouth to reply, but Heather was too worked up and steamrolled right over whatever he'd been about to say. "You wouldn't. Not at all, man. You'd want to lie low and be fucking inconspicuous. Shit!"

She stomped the Chevelle's floorboard with the heel of a boot.

Josh's expression became worried. "Hey...calm down, all right?"

Heather heaved another big sigh. "I just hate stupid people."

"I know. Stupid people suck."

Heather was nodding. "They should all die."

"Yep. Totally agree." Josh sounded more than a little nervous when he cleared his throat. "So...are we gonna do this thing or not?"

Heather glanced at the loaded .38 clutched tightly in her white-knuckled right hand and felt her chest grow tight. "I can't believe I'm doing this again. I swore I wouldn't."

Josh shrugged, smiling weakly. "Hey, I'm against it, remember? You want to call it off, that's cool by me."

Heather was shaking her head before she finished. "No. We need money. Now." She opened the door on her side and swung one long leg out of the car. She glanced at Josh. "Get behind the wheel and start the engine. I'm gonna make this fast, so be ready to go."

Josh gulped. His eyes were shining with fear now. "Okay."

"And don't blaze up."

He nodded. "Yeah. Okay."

Heather slithered out of the car and started quickly across the parking lot, a lean, long-legged, hip-swiveling slice of black-clad beauty. A stiff breeze stirred platinum-blonde hair. Stylish black shades hid eyes a startling shade of blue. A purse with a long strap hung from her right shoulder. Not so stylish, but it was right for the job. The hand gripping the gun was shoved down inside it. The clerk behind the counter wouldn't see it until it was too late.

Her heart hammered in her chest.

I don't want to do this. Not again.

Three years ago she'd robbed a liquor store at gun point. Her boyfriend Craig had been the instigator that time. The motive that time had been "fun" rather than monetary. A highly risky piece of thrill-seeking. Craig was dead now, one of the many victims of the Flaherty Brothers Traveling Carnivale and Freakshow. She had hated him by the end, but there had been a time when she'd allowed herself to fall fully under his bad boy spell. It hadn't hurt that he'd been such a good-looking son of a bitch. For a short while, she'd gone along with any crazy idea that entered his twisted mind. Like doing an armed robbery just to have done it.

This was different.

Everything was different since the freakshow.

She almost never slept anymore. She was afraid to close her eyes for fear of seeing the horribly deformed monstrosities from the freakshow in her dreams. The coke habit she'd developed went a long way toward staving off sleep and the nightmares that came with it. The downside to that was that coke wasn't cheap. She and Josh moved around a lot. Staying in one place more than a week made her nervous. Josh did a bit of day labor here and there wherever they landed, but they were perpetually low on funds. Yet never so low as they were now. Today they didn't have a single penny between them. The time had come to take someone else's money. She didn't like it, but desperation had a way of narrowing your options down to the single grimmest one available. There would be time for regrets later, after her life had finally settled down. Until the memories of the freakshow at last began to fade.

But for now...

She pushed through the double doors at the front of the store and strode confidently inside. Except for the pimply clerk behind the counter, the store was empty, as she'd expected. The store was located off a sleepy exit just inside the South Carolina border. The area was sparsely populated and the store itself was a ramshackle relic from another age. There were no security cameras. Someone else would come along sooner or later. There was no way around that. But if she did this fast, she should be able to get gone long before that could become an issue.

She approached the counter, hips swaying, her most radiant smile in place.

The scrawny clerk swallowed a lump in his throat and stared at her tits.

She pulled out the gun and pointed it at his face. "All the money from the register. Now."

He blinked slowly and looked up at her face. "Huh?"

She screamed and shoved a wire rack of cigarette lighters off the counter. The fake Zippos clattered on the tiled floor. She shoved the gun's barrel against his forehead. "Open the fucking register or I swear to God I'll fucking kill you!"

He was shaking now. Tears leaked from his eyes.

"Do it!"

A trembling hand reached for the register.

A bell rang and Heather shrieked, nearly jumping out of her skin.

"Oops. Awkward."

Heather backed away from the register and wheeled slowly around, trying to keep both the clerk and the interloper in her vision. Actually, it was interlopers, plural. A young girl with shaggy, dyed-black hair and pale skin. Her male companion was slender and wore a shiny black shirt with a flame pattern on the front. It looked like the sort of thing you'd buy from Hot Topic. The girl had a totebag. A hand was dipped casually inside. The young man stared at the gun in Heather's hand, his eyes wide and radiating fear, but the girl only seemed amused. Heather glanced beyond them and saw an antique automobile parked in front of the store. A big red Galaxie 500. They must have driven up just as she was losing her cool with the clerk, which, by the way, had happened at a stupidly fast speed. She thought about Josh out there in the parking lot. The plan had been for him to lay on the horn if anyone came along. Probably he'd blazed up again and had passed out behind the steering wheel, the fucking idiot.

She pointed the .38 at the guy in the Hot Topic shirt. "Get yourself and your girl over here behind the counter. Don't make me—"

"Talk to me, not him."

Heather squinted at the girl. She was smirking. What the

hell was wrong with her? She wanted to smack the expression off her insolent face, but there wasn't time for that. "Whatever. Just do what I—"

The girl's hand came out of her totebag. "Oops. Look what I have."

Heather gaped in disbelief as the barrel of the girl's gun came up and pointed at her belly. This couldn't be happening. Not only was everything going wrong, it was going wrong in every most fucked up way possible. This was just insane. It was—

BAM!

The bullet punched through Heather's stomach, propelling her backward into a potato chip display. The bags went flying and Heather tumbled to the floor, the pain ripping at her as she rolled across the tiles. She tried to bring her own gun around to aim at the girl, but it had slipped from her fingers. She slapped at the floor tiles, grasping for the fallen weapon, but her fingers found only smears of her own blood. Heather cried out and lifted her head.

The girl was at the counter now, aiming the gun at the trembling clerk. He raised his hands in a pathetic warding-off gesture.

The guy in the Hot Topic shirt was shaking his head faster and faster. "Roxie, don't!"

BAM!

Blood exploded from the back of the clerk's head and he slumped ass-first to the floor. The girl strolled over to Heather and knelt down over her. She pressed the barrel of the gun against Heather's forehead and smiled. "Say goodnight."

Blood trickled from the corners of Heather's mouth. "No. No."

The girl's smile broadened. "Yes."

Heather never heard the killing shot.

Back on the highway now and behind the wheel of the Galaxie, Rob glanced at Roxie, who sat slouched in the shotgun seat. She was sucking on a lollipop, a serene expression on her face. "You didn't have to do that guy in the Chevelle. He was passed out."

She shrugged. "Didn't have to, no. That's one of the joys of life, Rob. You can spare a moment now and then for a bit of pointless pleasure. It's called freedom. You should revel in your freedom."

Rob felt sick as he stared at the empty road ahead. "You're crazy."

"That's not nice. Take it back."

"I'm sorry."

"It's okay. I forgive you. I am sort of crazy, after all."

Rob couldn't help it. He laughed. It was insane. Even in the face of such horror, she made him laugh. What was wrong with him? What was he becoming?

Roxie took the lollipop out of her mouth. "You know what the chick's mistake was?"

"What?"

"Hesitation. If you're gonna go around pointing guns at people, you gotta be ready to use them. She should have shot us the second she saw us, the dumb bitch. But she didn't. You know why?"

Rob shook his head again. He could guess, but there was no point. Roxie wanted to pontificate a bit and it was best to just let her go on without interruption. "Why?"

"Because she didn't have it in her. She wasn't a killer. Not like us."

"Like you, you mean."

Roxie smiled and slurped on the lollipop again. "Like us, I mean. We're the same, you just don't fully see it yet. You're the killing kind, baby. The sooner you admit it to yourself, the happier you'll be."

Rob shook his head and kept silent.

Maybe she was right.

The road ahead was long.

Sooner or later, he'd find out the truth about himself.

BRAIN WORMS CRAVE SOUL FOOD

The sheet of paper was as empty as a stormtrooper's soul, a white sliver of nothingness coiled like an impotent serpent in the old pawn shop typewriter. A ream of paper sat next to the rickety relic, four-hundred and ninety-nine more blank canvases.

Rafe Martin's fingers settled once again on the home row keys.

He could feel something swelling within him, a surge of creative energy, and his fingers tingled with the need to shape worlds with words, to journey to places within himself he could only reach via this strange alchemy/interaction of body, mind, and machine. His fingers depressed the keys slightly, the burgeoning need nearly achieving critical mass, but the drive to create ebbed, breaking like a wave on a shore, then finally receding altogether.

He sighed and slumped back in his chair.

A vein in his head throbbed, and he gingerly massaged it, working the fingers of his right hand in slow circles over warm flesh.

He frowned.

It felt like something was moving in there.

Probably just a tactile hallucination brought on by stress and lack of sleep

The frustration he felt at his continuing inability to fashion even one decent sentence was approaching a level dangerous to his mental well-being. Writing was his life's passion, but right now it was just a burden. He wanted the words to flow in a heady, mad rush of inspiration, the kind of stream-of-consciousness explosion of prose the old beat writers he so admired were famous for.

Rafe lit a cigarette.

He forced his gaze away from the blank sheet. The sun was slanting in through the partially open slats of the mini-blinds, providing the only illumination in the small second bedroom he'd converted into a workspace. He saw the tall spires of the city's skyline through a haze of smog and refracted light. The city was big and sprawling, a diverse amalgamation of clubs and restaurants, museums and theaters, businesses small and large. Even from here, through the deepening haze, it fairly pulsed with life and vitality.

With endless possibilities.

Rafe stubbed the cigarette out and lurched forward. His fingers pounced on the home row keys and he typed.

THE SLEEPING CITY
by Rafe Martin

The city was trauma. Skyscrapers stabbed the bleeding sky. The rain fell like God's final judgment, a wash of cleansing acid that scorched the flesh and made the sidewalks sizzle. Predator eyes followed a drowning man into a dive bar.

Blackness like an abyss.

Then, a rattle of glass and the shock of neon--

The door to the office creaked open and Rafe muttered a curse. He wheeled about in the swivel chair to face the intruder.

Balika.

She entered the room smiling and bearing a tray of food. Steaming, spicy Indian stuff that gave Rafe heartburn. The mere thought of ingesting any of it made his stomache rumble and his throat constrict.

Balika's smile was radiant. "A feast for my sweetie. A nice surprise for my hard-working man."

She set the tray down on the desk.

Rafe didn't look at the food.

An incipient fever burned behind his eyes, a wall of fear accompanied by a strange tingling along his hairline. If he didn't know better, he would swear a colony of fleas was nesting there. There was a faint sensation of…crawling.

Christ, he had to get to bed at a decent hour tonight.

He forced himself to look at the woman who professed to love him.

"There's this thing we Americans do prior to entering a room, Balika. We knock. It's considered an act of courtesy, a way of asking *permission* to enter a room."

Balika's hands went to her hips as she struck a defiant pose. "Listen buster, I pay the rent here. I pay the bills. I buy the groceries. Unless you want your unemployable butt thrown out on the street, you'll knock off the snide tone when talking to me."

Rafe spun away from her and sat facing the view of the city skyline again. Balika continued to rant, but the words barely registered, because he was now consumed with a need that exceeded even his drive to create (which, let's face it, hadn't been so strong lately); the need to be gone from this place.

To be somewhere far away from Balika.

The room suddenly felt stifling, confining, a pit of artistic stagnation. He spent too much time in this room. He needed to be *out there*, experiencing the city, filling himself up with the raw material he needed to become something more than a wannabe hack.

He started to rise from the chair, but he felt Balika's firm hands at his shoulders. She pushed him back down and turned him toward her. Her lovely brown skin looked darker than usual, flushed with the heat of her anger. Despite his own anger, something in Rafe reacted to her raw sensuality. His breathing grew shallow as thoughts of art and transcendence gave way to lust.

Balika was a twenty-three-year-old native of India whose family had moved to the states when she was a little girl. Rafe had met her at a party a year ago, a boring affair he'd been in the process of exiting when he spied her coming in. She was gorgeous, an exotic beauty with long, lustrous brown hair, a lithe, shapely body, soft skin, and the face of an eastern goddess. Never before had he felt so galvanized by the sight of a woman. She met his gaze at the door, smiled, and that was it.

He belonged to her.

How strange to feel the echo of that old feeling now, when the resentment he felt at his "kept man" status was peaking.

She slapped him.

The sting of her hand across his check anesthetized his libido.

"Balika--"

"Shut up." Her voice stung, a verbal slap. "I will come and go in my own home as I see fit, do you hear me?"

Rafe's shoulders sagged. "Yes."

Her gaze went to the typewriter, and an eyebrow rose as she spied the handful of words on the page. She stepped around Rafe, leaned over the desk, and read what he'd written.

She frowned. "Rafe, you write like a constipated Kerouac channeling Raymond Chandler, like a high school boy with a head full of dope and bad poetry. What the fuck does 'The city was trauma' mean?"

Rafe bristled. "It's a…metaphor."

Who the hell was she to criticize his work? She wasn't a writer. How dare she presume to tell him anything about artistic matters. She had no appreciation for the flow of language, for the rhythm of prose. She mistakenly believed a handful of college lit courses she'd aced lent her opinions an added authority.

His temple pulsed some more, the vein throbbing like a frayed power line. He felt something shift under the skin, a snake-like slither of movement that made his eyebrows twitch. He pressed the heel of a hand to his brow, vainly trying to ward off what promised to be one wicked bitch of a headache. The need to be away from Balika was back; her caustic commentary masquerading as "constructive criticism" was only making things worse.

She snorted. "Metaphor, my ass. It's non-sensical. It's crap."

Crap.

The word was like a roundhouse blow to his soul, more hurtful by far than the physical aggression of a few moments ago. It was just more evidence of how little she valued their relationship. The truth was she didn't want an equal partnership. He could point out all the countless times she'd dissuaded him from efforts to find a regular job, but what was the point? She used his current reliance on her against him, as a means of emasculating him, but the truth was she wanted things this way. She didn't want a boyfriend, really, or a fiancé or husband--she wanted a possession, a plaything.

She was like a grown-up little girl with a living, breathing doll.

Ken with a functional dick.

Rafe hadn't minded it much at first, but he'd grown weary of the situation. The sex was incredible, but he was starting to believe even that wouldn't be enough to keep him in this parasitic relationship much longer.

Rafe seethed.

There was just…one…little…problem…with that.

With her encouragement and support, he'd quit his job nearly a year ago to pursue his dream of writing full time. That, coupled with his spotty work history prior to meeting Balika, meant he'd have a hard time finding a job with a good enough income to live on his own. The situation was a classic Catch-22; he couldn't leave unless he found a good job, and Balika would threaten to kick him out and cut off her monetary support if he started hunting for a job.

Balika was smirking. She folded her arms under her breasts and gazed down at him, her lower lip pooched out in a mockery of a pout. "Oh, did I hurt your feelings, little Rafey? Should Mommy not be so blunt when appraising your…work?"

Rafe glared at her.

It was too much; she was pushing him too hard. "You…"

He struggled to breathe, righteous fury nearly consuming him.

"What was that, Rafey?" She cocked her head sideways and cupped a hand over her ear. More mockery. "I don't think I heard you. Were you…" Her hand came away from her ear and her face twisted itself into an expression of phony shock. "Oh my, Rafe, were you about to call me a bitch?" Her voice rose on the last word. "Or…or…no, you wouldn't call me a …*cunt*… would you?"

She gasped and covered her open mouth with her hands.

Rafe ground his teeth, the need to respond in kind, to lash out, was almost overwhelming. The boiling kettle of resentment he felt was about to spill over. Aside from the physical component of their relationship, he hated everything about her. He hated how Americanized she was, how freely she used profanity as a weapon. She maintained a pretense of sweetness until he showed a hint of backbone, then she unleashed a relentless furry of insults.

He gripped the armrests of his chair hard to still the shaking of his hands. His face flushed red and moisture, stress sweat, formed along his hairline.

Oh, how he wanted to make her eat those words.

But he couldn't.

He was hopeless.

Impotent.

Ineffectual.

Weak.

Tears or sweat, probably both, filled his eyes, and he was momentarily unable to see Balika's leering face. A blessing, perhaps. But then something moved again behind his forehead, a jarring physical/psychical slippage akin to the shifting of rock strata in an earthquake. His skull seemed to pulse outward, distending like an over-inflated balloon.

He heard a scream.

He wasn't sure of the source; could've been Balika letting loose, but maybe it was his own vocal cords producing that strangled burst of terror.

He felt the flesh around his eye sockets swell to unnatural proportions. There was something moving there, something flowing *out*. He pitched out of the chair, clamped his hands over his throbbing head, and screamed (no doubt of the source this time). He heard the clack of Balika's heels on the hardwood floor as she backpedaled away from him, heard her shrill, offended voice; "You asshole! You fucking asshole, Rafe! What the hell's wrong with you? Are you on drugs? Are you fucking high?" Then a groan as the realization that something far worse was happening. "Oh, fuck, don't you dare stroke out in my house, motherfucker! I'm not gonna take care of your crippled ass, you hear me?"

Rafe screamed again.

His head was a starburst of agony, ground zero for endless, consciousness-obliterating explosions of pain. His nasal passages expanded as something that pulsed heat pushed through them, stretching the skin thin, like a too-small condom rolled over a huge cock. It was the way ropes of molten shit might feel squirting out of his anus. He felt the heat emerge through his nostrils.

Then he could see again.

Twin strands of thick, pink tissue descended from his nose. Ropes of organic matter that twitched and strained. Rafe got a look at eyeless heads with thin-slit, hungry mouths. The things wriggled free of his noise, struck the floor with a wet *plop*, then darted toward Balika.

Now Balika screamed.

She turned to flee, but the brain worms--as Rafe instantly thought of them--were too fast, closing the gap instantly. Rafe saw them race up her bare legs. He shuddered at the sight of them moving under her dress, then again as they emerged through her cleavage and climbed into her mouth and nose. She swatted at the worms and shook her head in a frantic effort to dislodge them.

It was useless.

Her face and forehead swelled as the creatures coiled themselves inside her. She moaned and swayed on her feet as the worms continued to move inside her, jerking her flesh in various directions as they…did whatever they were doing.

Then she tumbled to the floor and lay flat on her back.

Rafe was too numb to feel horror, grief or anything else for several minutes. He was stunned by the blatant impossibility of what had just occurred. For a while, his mind flat-out refused to acknowledge the reality of the event. It was the kind of scenario dreamed up by hack horror writers going for cheap shocks. What he had just witnessed just didn't happen in the everyday, rational world.

And yet…it *had* happened.

Correction. It was *still* happening.

Although Balika's head was no longer twice its natural size, there was still movement around her frontal lobes that could only be described as "abnormal." Rafe sat there and watched the impossible, the absolutely fucking absurd, continued to exist.

He felt a surge of nausea.

Those…things…had been inside his own head. Nesting there. Hibernating. Waiting for just the right moment to emerge and…feed?...migrate? Whatever. The most pertinent questions at the moment were what were they and where the hell did they come from?

Whatever they were, they were external in origin, of that he was sure.

Well.

Pretty sure, anyway.

He knew human brains didn't normally function as nesting grounds for parasitic monster movie critters. He considered the possibility the brain worms were of extraterrestrial origin. Alien beings that subsisted on human brain matter. When they were through with one host, they simply moved on to another, as was apparently happening now.

He spotted the flaw in that theory right away.

He wasn't dead.

In fact, despite what he'd just endured, he seemed pretty healthy.

Balika, on the other hand…

Rafe gasped as the head of his lover/captor again contorted, the nostrils swelling like plastic tubes with pork being pushed through them. He saw the eyeless heads of the brain worms emerge, twitch, and seem to sniff the air. They wriggled the rest of the way out and began oozing across the floor toward Rafe.

He shrieked and scooted away from them.

His back struck the writing desk.

He saw them streak across the floor and slither over his jeans. He clawed at them as they plunged back into his nasal passages.

Then the world went white again.

And stayed that way for a while.

Rafe regained consciousness a short while later. He touched his head, feeling for unnatural protuberances, but there was nothing. He scanned the room, but there was no sign of the brain worms.

Balika was alive.

Her eyes were wide and white, staring at nothing.

Rafe conducted a careful search of the apartment before calling the emergency number. There was no indication of brain worms or anything else of a bizarre nature. When the paramedics arrived a little later, they determined Balika had suffered some sort of massive hemorrhage. The police subsequently checked for evidence of foul play, but there was nothing to suggest anything untoward happened.

Just an unfortunate tragedy.

Sometimes fate failed to smile on the young and healthy, as Balika's grieving mother put it during that first long night at the hospital.

His brain-fried lover's affluent parents arranged long-term care for Balika in a facility that specialized in comatose patients. A "veggie farm," as Rafe thought of it. Balika's father set up a trust fund in Rafe's name, deeming that his daughter's one true love should receive the generous inheritance that would have been hers had tragedy not struck.

Rafe also received a generous monthly allowance from Balika's father.

The old man called it an "investment," a way of validating his daughter's fervent belief in Rafe's potential as an artist.

For his part, Rafe entered the most productive phase of his writing "career." He turned out story after story of perfectly rendered, evocative portraits of life in India.

As viewed through the eyes of a young girl from that country.

The stories started selling.

Rafe was nominated for awards. A book contract was waiting to be signed.

Life should have been looking good.

But there was a potential wrench in the works, a complication that threatened to foul everything up. He was running on empty. If he hope to continue his career, the brain worms would have to feed again.

He knew what they were now.

Mutations.

Physical manifestations of his mind's creative component. He acknowledged now that he had no good ideas of his own. He had technical ability, but nothing more. So his mind had compensated, evolving a system through which he could absorb the knowledge and insights of others.

Pilfered gray matter.

Soul food.

He was some kind of super man.

A new super being, a new *species*.

But he wasn't a scientist, so he didn't give a shit about that.

One cold night at the end of October, he went out for a walk. He scanned the faces of passerby, searching their eyes for indications of something special--of an interesting life. He encountered many candidates, but none that quite galvanized him the way poor Balika had. Then he stepped into a bar to get out of the cold, an Irish pub filled with laughter and raucous music.

He took a seat at the end of the bar, ordered a pint of stout, and cast his gaze down the length of the bar.

His mouth opened.

His breath caught in his throat.

The pretty Vietnamese girl at the other end of the bar smiled at him.

Rafe's hand closed hard around the cold pint glass the barmaid placed in front of him.

The faint pulse at his temples made him shudder.

He picked up the beer and walked in a daze toward the other end of the bar.

Visions of rice paddies and bamboo huts danced in his head.

Yes, he thought, smiling.

A logical new direction.

Thinking about what the critics would make of his continued

explorations of eastern societies, he slid onto a stool next to the Vietnamese girl. She smiled again, and they struck up an easy, comfortable conversation.

Rafe almost felt sorry for her.

She didn't know it yet, but her life wasn't her own anymore.

Something flexed in his head.

He invited her to his place.

After a very brief hesitation, she accepted.

His conscience, so long ago left to atrophy and die, sputtered faintly, dimly pleading with him not to let this happen.

He almost listened to it.

Almost.

He held her coat for her as she slipped it on.

Then they left the warmth of the bar for the cold of the city street.

RATTLEHEAD

Ray Webber was thinking about killing Rattlehead. The guy just wouldn't shut the fuck up.

"Have you ever really thought about this song? I mean seriously thought about it?"

The song was CCR's "Have You Ever Seen the Rain." The oldies station Ray's car radio was tuned to was playing it. "No." Ray kept his voice neutral—he was in no mood to hear one of Rat's diatribes. "Can't say I have."

"Listen to this bullshit."

They listened to it.

Ray kind of liked the song. It was innocuous, just a pleasant old noise on the radio. But Rattlehead was the kind of guy who found something to bitch about in everything.

"Have I ever seen the rain?" Rat's voice was tinged with sarcasm. "Yes John, I have seen the rain. I've seen the snow and the fucking ice too. What about it, pinhead?"

Ray sighed. "I think it's about Vietnam. The social upheaval of the sixties. Like a metaphor."

Rat groaned. "Metaphor, shmetaphor. You're thinking about the other one, where's he's asking who'll stop the shit."

"Whatever."

Ray turned the volume up when a station promo segued into a Stone's song. The urge to kill Rat was beginning to move out of the realm of pure fantasy, acquiring more of the weight of reality every time the fucker opened his mouth. He thought about the aluminum baseball bat in the trunk. A few blows to the head ought to do the job. Rat would never know what hit him.

"This song's a load of shit!" Rat yelled, pitching his voice at a level much higher than the music. "Just your nineteenth nervous breakdown! The language belies the seriousness of mental illness!"

His real name was Sloan Walker. He was a man who had no tolerance for the dead spaces in conversations. He labored to fill every spare second of silence, never failing to voice an opinion on anything that entered his warped sphere of experience. A self-anointed ultimate arbiter of the Final Word on anything that mattered, he viewed the world with an unblinking wide-angle lens.

He was a pain in the ass.

His friends called him Rattlehead because of all the useless bits of information that were rattling about in his head. Some shortened the nickname, calling him Rat. This wasn't a term of endearment.

Ray strove to remember a time when he'd genuinely liked Rat. Maybe when they had been kids, back in the days when they had shared with their friends a penchant for getting into trouble. Pranksters with a sense of humor, they had been the scourge of the community. People back home still talked about the time some goddamn vandals stole a huge Budweiser balloon from a convenience store and deposited it on the mayor's lawn.

Rat's idea, of course.

That kind of thing had been mucho fun in those bygone adolescent halcyon days. Now, though, all their old running mates were certified grown-ups. Ray himself was on the verge of crossing the three-oh threshold, and he hoped to achieve a state of dignified adulthood someday soon. But Rat was content to maintain a state of arrested adolescence indefinitely.

Look at what he'd done in that Nashville bar last night. The crazy fucker downed a few beers, went to the bathroom, and emerged moments later stark naked. To the disbelief of the shocked patrons, Rat thumped his chest, emitted a Johnny Weismuller-like bellow, and then bolted through the dining area and out the front door. A girl at the bar remarked on the possible significance of the old Ted Nugent lyrics he had been hollering on his way out

"Wasn't that the "Great White Buffalo?" Ya think he's making some kinda statement?"

Ray hadn't known what to say to that.

Rat latter explained that he'd decided to do his part to make streaking popular again. "This AIDS shit has people so goddamn uptight. I'm tired of being so desperate for a safe piece of ass. So I had an epiphany. I realized life is too goddamn short to worry about disease and bad shit like that. I figured people need to start having fun again. Loosen up, hence my decision to bring back streaking."

It made a twisted kind of sense. Ray was frightened to have found even the thinnest thread of logic in anything Rat said. The guy was a maniac. Certifiable.

So why did he still hang out with him?

Inertia.

Maybe that was it. Ray had always been content to just be. He didn't strive to understand the nature of things. He didn't need explanations. Things just were. Rat was just the opposite. But they were alike in one important way—neither had ever accomplished anything of significance.

Inertia.

Probably.

So Ray was beginning to think maybe things should change. Maybe he should get a real job. Go back to school. Work toward building a solid future. To do that, though, he would have to jettison some excess baggage.

Kill him.

If he told the guy to take a permanent hike, he'd disappear for a few weeks before eventually showing up again. Ray knew this from sad experience. The guy was like a damn yo-yo, always bouncing back.

Inertia.

Ray was sick of the bastard.

Sick of his own go-nowhere life.

Sick to death of listening to this kind of shit: "Have you ever noticed how people don't really fight in bars? They push and shove, they throw shit, but you almost never see anybody actually beat the living shit out of anybody. Like that time you—"

"FUCK IT!"

Rat glanced at him. "Something wrong, Raymond?"

Ray cupped the back of Rat's head with his right hand, stepped hard on the brake pedal, and gave the pest a shove. Rat's forehead smacked the windshield, cracking the glass and opening a gash above one eye. Blood streamed sideways down his face as his unconscious form slumped against the door. He looked like the loser of a heavyweight title bout.

Ray drove without thinking for a few minutes. A Doors song played on the radio.

Ray listened.

People are strange.

No kidding.

Ray made sure the odometer needle stayed a hair over sixty-five. Traffic was light on this lonely stretch of rural interstate—and he was certain there had been no witnesses—but he knew a heightened sense of caution would enhance his chances of getting away with this.

He needed to assess the situations, formulate step by careful step a plan that would bring about a successful resolution to this crisis.

Take him to a hospital.

Maybe.

He could tell the authorities he'd panicked when a dog had darted into the road. Rat's recollection of the incident would be clouded by the trauma he'd endured. He might not remember anything. Maybe everything could be safely returned to normality. Maybe…

Maybe a lot of things.

Especially this—maybe Ray didn't want things returned to normal. Maybe he favored the part of himself that saw what he had done as a bold first step in the right direction. Stagnant Ray wasn't capable of momentous acts. Life-changing acts. Maybe it was time Bold Ray excised his sickly other half for good.

He glanced at Rat.

He was still out.

Still quiet.

Ray realized how much he hoped he would never have to listen to the fucker again.

"Fuck it."

He drove another eight miles, found the exit he was looking for, and left the interstate. He negotiated the familiar maze of rural back roads with a mounting sense of unease. Not many cops cruised back here, but the ones who did sometimes pulled you over for the pure hell of it. He didn't begin to relax until he found the deserted boat dock he remembered from youthful excursions. He drove to the edge of the short, sloping pier, shut off the engine, and surveyed the area.

Nobody around.

As usual.

The unpopular dock was in a shallow cove accessible only to smaller boats. There was a boarded-up shack that had once been an unprofitable bait shop. He got out of the car and walked over to the decrepit structure. A rusted padlock dangled from an equally rusty latch. He gave the door a hard kick, and the latch popped out of the rotting wood. He took a good look inside. There wasn't much to see.

Snatches of memory crowded Ray's mind, images of drunk kids whose lives were filled with too much idle time and who were blissfully unaware of any better way to spend that time. The shack had been one of Rat's favorite hangouts in the old days. It seemed appropriate that the guy who never wanted to grow up would spend his last moments in a place that remained one of the emotional touchstones of his short life.

"Raymond!"

Ray breathed a curse.

Rattlehead.

"Come out, come out, wherever you are, fuckhead!"

Ray relaxed a bit—no way would Rat be in any condition to mount a successful defense of his life.

Right?

Ray strode out of the shack in the grip of a sense of purpose as strong as anything he'd ever experienced. Old Ray would have avoided this confrontation.

Fuck that shit.

New Ray stepped into a blow from an aluminum baseball bat. The end of the bat clipped the tip of his chin, caused him to stagger back into the shack.

Rat followed him.

"You're a stupid fucker, Raymond."

Ray gave his head a hard shake.

Focus.

He back away from his slowly advancing adversary. The guy had surprised him, granted, and he was armed and relatively dangerous. Chalk up two minor points for the opposition. But Rat was still damaged goods. He had a weapon, but he didn't have the strength to wield it effectively. The one blow he'd manage to deliver thus far had been no more painful than a bee sting.

"I can't believe how unutterably dumb you are, Raymond." Blood was still seeping from the gash above Rat's eye. "You didn't think this through. You wanna off somebody, never make the mistake of acting on impulse. That's the downfall of a lot of would-be killers."

"Yeah?"

Keep him talking.

"You'd know that shit if you read True Detective. You'd know not to let your emotions dictate your actions. You've already fucked up about a thousand different ways."

Rattlehead still loved to talk.

Maybe for once he had something to say worth hearing.

"How have I fucked up, Sloan?"

Rat rolled his bleary eyes. "You've left a motherfucker of an evidence trail. There's blood all over the front seat. Blood on the windshield. And that's just the physical evidence. Think about all the people we met last night. We're talking dozens of witnesses. There's everybody back home—hell, I can think of at least a half dozen people who know we went to Nashville together."

Ray thought about it.

A knot of tension formed in his gut.

Christ!

He had been so sure he was doing everything right. But there were so many things he hadn't considered at all. He needed some kind of cover story. Some—

Shit!

Rat lunged at him

Ray sidestepped the blow, snatched the bat away from Rat, and waited until his attacker turned around. This part of it went exactly as he'd envisioned it. The bat thumped the side of Rat's head, and he fell to the ground.

Rat was quiet again.

Everything became clear again.

Ray went back to the car, where he found the keys still lodged in the trunk lock. He put the bat in the trunk and replaced the keys in the ignition. Then he returned to the shack, got a good grip on Rat's wrists, and dragged him back to the car. After successfully completing the heavy lifting part of the job, Ray started the car, put it in reverse, and allowed it to drift back to the foot of the pier.

He had a simple plan—put the car in neutral, guide it to the end of the pier, and bail out at the last moment. Let the lake swallow the evidence. There was a good possibility it would eventually be discovered, but he should be able to concoct a believable cover story before that happened. There would be time enough to think that part of it through once this thing was done.

So do it.

He tapped the gas pedal, and the car began to crawl along the creaky pier. He moved the gearshift to neutral, grasped the door handle with one shaky hand, and listened to his heart slam as the Civic picked up speed.

"This is brilliant, Raymond." Rat was conscious again. "How're you getting back?"

Ray frowned.

Goddammit.

His hand hovered over the gearshift.

The fuck is wrong with my brain today?

Rat was giggling. "I'll grant you this, Raymond, you're

reliable—just when I figured you can't get any dumber, you go and prove me wrong. Never fails. Hell, you're not even considering the motherload of bad karma you're accumulating."

Karma?

Ray scowled. "That's hippie bullshit."

So he bailed out. He had been about to stop the car and attempt to come up with a new strategy, but Rat had opened his huge fucking mouth one time too many. The car hit the water nose first, sank a few feet, the tipped over onto its roof. Ray caught a glimpse of Rat through the sliver of window still visible above the waterline; he wasn't trying to get out. Maybe he'd finally succumbed to the damage done by the blows he'd sustained.

He hoped not.

Rat should suffer some more.

A lot more.

Ray endured several terrifying minutes during which he became convinced the car wasn't going to sink. The thing just bobbed along there like a child's toy floating in a bathtub. Then a muffled thud was followed by the vehicle's shockingly rapid submission. Air bubbles suddenly dotted the water's murky surface.

Had Rat kicked out a window?

Ray groaned.

Moron.

That's what Rat would say.

Shoulda rolled down the window.

He waited until the air bubbles disappeared, then he turned away from Rat's final resting place and began to walk away. A sense of exhilaration pumped extra adrenaline into his system, made him giddy.

I did it!

So he had.

But the thrill of accomplishment began to ebb almost immediately. There were too many things to think about now, too many potential complications he would have to recognize and confront. Unpleasant scenarios of apprehension and punishment assailed him. He imagined a prosecutor telling a jury about the thousand different ways he'd fucked up. By the time he reached the road, he was rehearsing what he would say when the appeals ran out and the prison chaplain asked him if he had any last words.

Yeah, I did the world a goddamn favor.

He'd walked a half mile due east without encountering a single soul when a Chevy pickup appeared in the distance. He smoothed back his dirty hair, stuck out a thumb, and hope he didn't look like a psycho.

The Chevy slowed as it neared him. A big redneck bubba was behind the wheel. Seated next to him was his identical twin. Well, they look like twins. Visions of Ned Beatty in Deliverance flashed through Ray's mind.

But they didn't stop.

Ray figured that was a good thing. They did, however, toss half-empty cans of Old Milwaukee at him.

This was a bad thing.

The front of his new shirt was soaked with cheap beer and redneck saliva.

He didn't know which was worse.

Ray decided he was going to kill the poor fucker who eventually picked him up.

What the hell?

He saw things this way.

Rat was right.

He had done every goddamn thing completely fucking wrong, and he didn't have a chance in hell of getting away with it. And he knew of no good reason to stick around and face the consequences. There was a simple way out. Kill some schmuck, take his car, and head out to the highway. Change the plates, get a new look, and disappear somewhere. Maybe make a new life on the coast.

Hell, he could do anything.

He was so immersed in his fantasies that he wasn't aware of the cruiser creeping up on him until it was too late. He froze when he saw the familiar blue and white markings.

"Oh, shit."

A big cop built like a pro linebacker got out of the car,

instructed Ray to assume the position, and drew his gun when Ray didn't immediately obey.

"ASSUME THE GODDAMN POSITION!"

Ray leaned against the car, endured a maddeningly thorough frisk, and weighed the pros and cons of trying to kill an armed man built like a T-Rex.

He decided against it.

When the cop was satisfied Ray wasn't packing, he put him in the back of the cruiser. Then he got behind the wheel, put the car in gear, and drove away.

"Am I under arrest?"

The cop chuckled.

Ray tried to sound calm. "I don't think this is standard police procedure. Aren't you supposed to—"

"Shut the fuck up." The cop's stern voice reminded Ray of his high school principal. "I don't like jabberjaws."

Ray grunted.

Neither do I.

They rode in silence for a while. Then the cop made a left turn down a narrow gravel road. Ray knew the road—he'd made the same turn less than an hour ago.

We're going to the boat dock.

Ray figured this was the part of the movie where the hero made his mad dash to freedom. Things looked grim, and it was up to Mel Stallone to save the freakin' day.

Ray reached for the door handle.

One problem.

There wasn't a door handle.

Ray groaned.

Fuckin' cop car.

The cruiser came to a stop next to the former bait shop. The cop got out of the car, opened the rear door for Ray, and instructed him to get the hell out.

Ray did as he was told.

"W-why did you bring me here?"

The cop grinned.

Ray was sure some unseen witness—a meddlesome lurker in the nearby woods—had reported his crime to the cops. Why else would he have been brought here? Then again, maybe this had nothing to do with Rat's murder.

This prospect was somehow more frightening. The cop's next words cranked his fear up yet another notch.

"I get bored."

Then he unsheathed his nightstick, prodded Ray with it, and directed him toward the shack.

"Get in there, bitch."

Ray trembled.

Bitch?

When they were inside the shack, the cop told him to walk to the center of the room, then turn around and get on his knees. Ray did as he was told. He had no choice, he could only hope he possessed the strength to endure whatever foul thing the cop had in mind.

The cop grinned. "How do you like my pad?"

"Ummm…"

Maniac Cop laughed. "This is a dull damn job boy. I'd go crazy if I didn't have my little home away from home."

"Ummm…"

The cop unzipped his fly.

Ray's heart sank.

He had been hoping for a beating.

"I think you know the drill, boy."

Ray guessed he did.

"You don't wanna disappoint me."

Ray did his best.

When it was over, the cop took him back outside. "We're gonna walk down to the pier." The nightstick poked his back. "You hear me?"

Ray nodded.

They kept going when they reached the pier. The cop kept poking him with the nightstick. Ray kept thinking about what Rat had said about accumulating bad karma. What a major goddamn understatement.

This was a karma neutron bomb.

The cop told him to stop when they reached the end of the pier. Ray supposed he would've kept on going if he hadn't been told otherwise.

Not that it mattered.

Hell, the water almost looked inviting.

The cop sheathed his nightstick, unholstered his gun, and said, "Any last words?"

Ray thought about it. "Nah. Fuck it."

The cop shot him once in the back.

It hurt like a son of a bitch.

The blast propelled him off the pier, and he was momentarily airborne. Then the water was rushing to meet him, and he accepted the bracing cold slap of its embrace with equal degrees of fear and acceptance.

He sank.

He saw a lot of scary things on the way down.

Body parts.

Bones.

Rattlehead.

His old friend had almost managed to escape from the sinking car. His left foot was caught in the crumpled steering wheel. The rest of his body floated outside the ruined vehicle, arms outstretched, head lolling to the side, He looked like an underwater scarecrow.

Ray saw these things too clearly.

He shouldn't be able to see at all down here.

Then he understood.

He was already dead.

He studied his dead friend's face more closely.

The bastard was smiling crookedly, an all too familiar taunt. *Welcome to hell, genius*, the smile seemed to say. *Guess you fucked up again. What a freakin' surprise.*

Ray could hear the implied words echoing in his head, and his mouth opened in a silent scream. Water that tasted like an odd mix of semen and cheap beer flooded his dead lungs. He dug his nails into his scalp, shredding dead flesh and releasing a steady stream of blood that drifted upward into the distant light. But the flesh began to heal almost instantly, and he knew this fevered attempt to free his tortured brain from its moorings was doomed.

Like me, Ray thought.

Doomed to taste cheap beer and cum forever. Doomed to never hear again anything but Rattlehead's mocking words and strangely satisfied laughter. But a simple truth bothered Ray more than any of these tortures—even in death, even here in hell, nothing much has fucking changed.

Except that Rat's laughter was growing even louder.

TRUTH

This is a dream. No question this horrid thing *isn't* happening. Kyle Miller is aware of this on an intellectual level. But his dream life has achieved such an advanced state of lucidity that the gruesome imagery often seems more real than the world of his waking life.

In the dream, he is in a stranger's apartment. A skinny blonde girl in her early twenties is tied to the headboard of a king-sized bed. There's a rag stuffed in her mouth and a strip of duct tape covers it.

There is a knife in Kyle's right hand.

A big, gleaming knife with a nasty-sharp blade.

The dream Kyle climbs onto the bed and begins the slow process of flaying every inch of flesh from the girl's body. It is what he always does with his dream victims. There is no sexual component to this obsession. At least there is no bodily evidence of arousal.

He does not rape his victims. Instead, the need that drives him to do these vile things is more esoteric.

He needs to see what his victims look like without their flesh.

Needs to bear witness to the truth beneath the flesh.

When he thinks about this in his waking life, the idea strikes him as simultaneously repulsive and absurd. There is no great "truth" to be exposed by skinning innocent people alive. But the dream Kyle exists only to do this thing. He sees himself as a servant of truth. Flesh is a façade, a barrier to knowledge and understanding. When the flesh is gone, he learns.

He grows stronger and more powerful.

The exposed organs and sinew speak to him in a language only a being as uniquely informed as Kyle can interpret. He has become so skillful at extracting truth that his subjects are often still alive after the last strip of flesh has been peeled away.

This is what he strives to achieve, anything else is failure.

Kyle the observer, the real Kyle, suspects the dream Kyle's ideal isn't achievable in the real world. But in this dream, Kyle the seeker, the dream Kyle, observes the flayed girl's inner workings until he senses her body is about to give up the fight. He gleans what knowledge he can from this observation. Then he uses the knife to free her still-beating heart from the chest cavity.

The taste of it in his mouth is sublime.

Then he wakes up.

Kyle's eyes snapped open, blinking at the early morning semi-gloom filling the room. The clock on his nightstand gave the time as 5:41 a.m., which was a little more than a quarter hour before the alarm was set to trigger him out of sleep.

Carol, his wife of twelve years, slept soundly next to him. In a little over fifteen minutes, the alarm would snap her awake and she would lurch out of bed to go wake up the kids and start getting them ready for school.

Kyle's eyes misted with tears even as he smiled at the image. He loved them all dearly and would lay down his life for them without hesitation. They were everything to him. There were times when he wished something would happen to take him away from them, something beyond his control life like a heart attack or a freak auto accident. A suicide would negate much of the insurance, and he couldn't stomach the idea of leaving his family with less than what they deserved.

Still, he wished he could die.

For their sakes.

He was a monster. His very existence endangered them.

The murder dreams had plagued him for years, since the early part of his college career. Before he met Carol. And long before Joshua and little Angela had come along to brighten up his life. The dreams had become more frequent over the last several months, and he'd been having them nightly for weeks.

The increased frequency of the dreams was bad enough, but the dreams were longer now, more vivid and more detailed. Feature films instead of short, grainy loops. The skinny blonde from the latest had seemed as real to him as his wife.

He was spooked by the sudden conviction that the dream girl existed, that she was walking around somewhere out there in the flesh and blood world, just waiting for the day when Kyle Miller would shrug off his inhibitions and come to her in the night to slice away all that lovely, tanned skin.

I've got to end this, he thought.

Got to find a way out of this madness.

But how?

Death via some external means seemed the best option. It would eliminate him as a threat to both his family and society at large. If suicide was out as an option, he could pay someone to kill him. Have it done so it looked like the byproduct of a crime, a robbery gone wrong, something like that.

He saw the potential complications immediately. For one thing, he had no idea how to go about setting something like that up. He didn't know the sort of people who would kill a man for money. And the prospect of finding a suitably shady character to do the deed seemed like more trouble than it was worth.

So strike another option.

The next most obvious solution made his heart ache and filled him with dread. He glanced again at his wife. He knew she loved him and the children. She was happy. She had a home, a family, a husband with a job that afforded them a comfortable lifestyle.

She would be devastated and mystified if he filed for divorce.

So Kyle set that idea aside, too. For the moment. He would hold it in reserve as a last resort, an escape hatch he could utilize if his mental health took a dramatic turn for the worse—or if he ultimately failed to come up with a viable alternate solution.

The only other option he could think of was professional

help. Seeing a shrink was what most people would consider the sensible thing to do. But Kyle was terrified by the notion of allowing anyone to know about his dreams. He didn't talk about them with Carol. He'd never discussed them with anyone at all.

He was a good man.

A decent, honest, hard-working man.

A good parent and role-model with impeccable values.

At least, that was his image in the community. He was proud of that image, and he worked every day to uphold it. He couldn't stand the idea of that image being tainted. Sure, divorcing his loving wife and abandoning his kids would damage his reputation, but not nearly as much as being outed as a closet sicko.

Which left…nothing.

For the moment, he was out of ideas.

The alarm went off.

Carol yawned and sat up.

Kyle feigned a yawn and rolled over to switch off the alarm. An hour later, he was at work, where he was able to forget about his problems for a little while.

He dozed off on his lunch hour. A round of extraordinarily dull morning meetings about procedural matters concluded just before noon, and he retreated to his office, where he folded his arms on the desk and put his head down for a quick nap.

He experienced a jarring reentry into the nightmare world. He saw his own gloved hand peeling away the scalp of yet another young girl. He heard her muffled scream through the gag and duct tape. Her wide eyes looked up at him with unadulterated terror, the big white orbs dancing wildly in their sockets.

The door to his office opened and he jerked awake with a gasp.

Ann Slattery strode into his office without asking permission to enter. She threw the door shut and plopped into the chair opposite Kyle. This was typically thoughtless behavior for Ann, who, at forty, was not only the company's first female CEO, she was its youngest ever. Though she had a very cool, buttoned-down public persona, she was extremely attractive in a very icy way.

He wondered how good she'd look with the flesh stripped off those high cheekbones. The stray thought startled him. It was the first time he'd even fleetingly entertained an idea like that outside of his dreams.

Still…he couldn't shake the image.

He sensed something long-dormant uncoil inside him as he allowed the image to breathe in his mind. He saw Ann tied to a bed. The bed was in a room that was very tastefully, and expensively, decorated. It was how he imagined the bedroom of a woman like Ann Slattery must look. He grew hard as he pictured himself climbing onto the bed with the big knife in hand.

Ann squinted at him. "Kyle, are you all right?"

Kyle blinked.

"Yeah…yeah…I'm okay. Sorry. What's up?"

Ann frowned. "You had me worried. For a second there, you looked like a drooling headcase in a mental ward."

Kyle forced a smile. He tried to make a joke of it. "I'm perfectly sane. But now that you mention it, I could use a dose or two of lithium."

Ann rolled her eyes. "Seinfeld, you're not. Listen, I want you to have dinner with me tonight."

Now it was Kyle's turn to frown. "Are we entertaining prospective clients? I thought there was nothing on the calendar for the next few days."

Ann stared at him for a while. Her pale blue, intense eyes unnerved him. At last, she said, "That's what you can tell your wife."

Kyle flinched.

Ann's gaze never wavered.

Kyle fidgeted in his chair. He felt sweat form along his hairline and in his armpits. The CEO of the company was propositioning him. It was unethical and risky. And yet, she seemed as supremely confident as ever. It distressed him.

Ann sighed. "You're about to miss your chance. I'd like an answer *now*, Kyle."

It occurred to him there was a possibility he might really get to see the inside of Ann's bedroom tonight.

He swallowed hard.

And he said, "Okay."

Ann smiled. "Good boy." She rose from the chair and glanced at her watch. "I've got another meeting in a few minutes. But we'll work out the details later today, okay?"

Kyle nodded.

He felt numb.

Ann walked out of the office and closed the door behind her.

Kyle loosened his tie. "Oh my god."

And he thought, *I can't be thinking what I'm thinking.*

I can't be about to cheat on my wife.

That was bad enough, but even more disturbing was the memory of the fantasy he'd had about enacting his dream-world perversions on Ann. He'd long been convinced there was no sexual element to the strange obsession. The dreams were about achieving some weird state of elevated consciousness via an even weirder brand of murder alchemy. And yet, there was no denying the blatant sexual aspect of the Ann fantasy. And could it be just coincidence that his dream victims were always attractive young girls?

And always slender.

Always blonde.

Sweet, delectable nymphs.

Kyle felt sick.

He'd been deluding himself all along. Not only that, but his long-suppressed sick desires seemed to be surging to the surface.

He thought, W*hen I see Ann again, I'll tell her I've changed my mind.*

Yes.

And later in the week he'd get with a lawyer and file the divorce paperwork. The way he saw it, the level of danger to his family had just increased dramatically. He couldn't afford to procrastinate any longer, he had to take himself out of their lives.

Permanently.

In which case…well, maybe seeing Ann tonight would be okay.

He remained sitting in his chair long after lunch was technically over. Misery engulfed him as he contemplated the hopelessness of his situation.

There was no way out.

No possibility of escape whatsoever.

He stared at the black screen of his computer monitor. He wasn't sleepy, but he was zoning out. He was aware of no conscious decision to slip back into the fantasy.

But at some point he stopped seeing the computer monitor.

He saw himself in Ann's bedroom.

With the knife pressed to her hairline.

Fresh tears leaked from his eyes even as the fantasy progressed.

Kyle spent the rest of the work day mired in a state of frustrating indecision. One moment he would resolutely declare to himself that he could not, under any circumstances whatsoever, ever allow himself to be alone with Ann. He doubted he would actually kill her should she entice him to her home after dinner, but there was no reason to tempt fate by putting himself in that situation.

But the events of Ann's proposition and the sudden intrusion of the dreamland blood mania in his waking life combined to overwhelm his inhibitions. He not only wanted to go out to dinner with Ann, he wanted to see her sans clothes, wanted to lick every inch of her luscious body. He wanted to throw her down on the nearest available flat surface and fuck the living shit out of her.

Sure, he could do that.

And it would just be sex.

He wouldn't kill her. It was absurd to even think that.

Perhaps. Or perhaps not.

Inevitably, as he went round and round on the subject, he would be faced with an unpleasant reality. Regardless of whether Ann would survive a sexual encounter with him, he would be an adulterer.

Something he'd always believed was no step below pond scum.

Thinking this, he would experience a flush of shame.

But his thoughts always returned to Ann and what he wanted to do to her.

He would plead with God to make the images go away.

Prayers that went unanswered.

The day was nearly over. There was just one scheduled meeting left on the day's agenda. A budget meeting. Ann would be there. He was sure she'd try to catch him alone after it was over.

Kyle rose from his chair, snapped shut his briefcase, and walked out of the office. He took an elevator to the ground floor, nodded at the guard on duty at the security desk, and strolled through the lobby until he exited the building and stepped into the late afternoon sunshine.

He got in his car and drove away.

He was probably committing career suicide. He was expected to be at that meeting. Vanishing without a trace wasn't something that could be easily explained.

Not that it mattered.

He wasn't going back there, anyway.

The realization made him laugh. Not because it was funny. There was clearly no humor to be found in this insane thing he was doing. He didn't even know precisely what he was doing. He only knew he wasn't going back to work and he wasn't going home.

As he steered the car down the interstate ramp, a rush of fear made his shudder. This was the end result of a long struggle, yes, but until today he'd managed to live his life normally. He'd succeeded in holding the darkness within him in check. The dizzying, precipitous speed of his mental decline unsettled him.

So he had to go.

He was depriving his family of its provider, so he felt some guilt over that. But Carol was a strong woman. She had many people who cared for her and the kids. They would have a support system. They would be okay.

And, with him gone, they would be safe.

He drove and drove down the interstate. He didn't stop until he pulled off the highway to refuel at a convenience store a hundred miles east of home. The stop helped him focus. Okay, so he was diving headfirst off the deep end, but there were some practicalities to consider. He needed money. He already had a substantial amount in his wallet, but he would need more. At some point tomorrow he'd have to stop at a bank branch and make a withdrawal. Not enough to harm the family's finances, but enough to keep him comfortable for a while.

And then…well, he didn't know what would happen after that.

He could go to a Wal-Mart and buy a tent and some other supplies, whatever he needed to live off alone in the wilderness somewhere. The idea was a little nutty. He'd never been the survivalist type. But the more he thought about it, the more it appealed to him.

He could do it.

It was his duty as a human being. As long as he drew breath, he was a danger to anyone he encountered. Therefore, he would send himself into exile.

Back on the road, he continued to drive through the night.

After a few more hours had passed, he realized how exhausted he was, mentally and physically. He had to get off the road. So he started scanning the dark roadside for a green sign with lodging icons.

He saw something else first.

His headlights picked out a solitary figure on the roadside. A small person in baggy clothes and a cap with the brim pulled down over the top half of his face. Kyle was surprised to find himself slowing down and he watched the slow-moving man, who also had a duffel bag slung over his shoulder.

The person turned in his direction.

And stuck out a thumb.

Kyle felt his mouth go dry as he pulled over to the shoulder. He didn't know why he was doing this. He felt like a pawn being manipulated on the chessboard of fate. This was his role to play in the great mystery of life, and he had no choice in the matter.

He thumbed a button and the passenger side window slid down.

The hitchhiker hefted his duffel bag and came running up to the car. Then he leaned down to smile at Kyle through the open window. "Hey, sweetie. Givin' me a ride?"

Kyle swallowed a lump in his throat. The hitchhiker wasn't a man after all. The baggy clothes and the ballcap had effectively disguised her gender.

"How far are you going?"

"As far as you can take me."

Kyle leaned across the seat and popped open the door.

The girl hitchhiker dumped her duffel bag into the back and slid into the passenger seat. She pulled the door shut and offered her hand to Kyle. "I'm Lindy. That's short for Melinda."

Kyle shook her hand. "I'm Kyle."

Then he put the car in gear and pulled away from the shoulder. He glanced at Melinda and felt sick as he got a look at the wisps of blonde hair sticking out from under the ballcap.

She smiled again. "So, Kyle, where are you going?"

He shrugged. "I don't know."

An odd thing to say. The kind of statement that should arouse suspicion.

But her smile didn't falter. "Nothing wrong with that. I don't know where I'm going, either. I'm just seeing the country while I'm young and free."

She liked to talk. That much was obvious already.

"Can you at least tell me what you do, Kyle? You look like a successful guy. Nice car, nice clothes…wedding ring on your finger."

"I'm a truth-seeker, Lindy." Another odd thing to say.

She laughed. "So am I, Kyle, so am I."

He sounded solemn when he spoke again. "I'm on a journey. I don't know where I'm going. I don't know what'll happen. I'm in the midst of a process of self-discovery. Somewhere along the way, maybe, I hope, I'll find that great truth I'm looking for."

"Well, I wish you luck in your mission, Kyle." She yawned. "Jeez, I'm so tired."

"You're welcome to stay with me tonight." He laughed nervously when he saw her raised eyebrow. "I'll get you your own room, if you like."

She frowned. "Why would you do that, Kyle?"

He tried to sound nonchalant. "Because I've been on the road alone for a while. I like your company. Like you said, I'm successful. I can afford an extra room, no problem."

She seemed to relax. "Cool. Whatever. You don't have to get an extra room. Just don't try any funny stuff." A mischievous grin brightened her already pretty face. "Unless I ask you to, of course."

Kyle smiled.

He checked them into a motel a few miles down the road. One room.

While Lindy took her first shower in days, Kyle went back out. He bought some more supplies at an all-night convenience store. When he returned, he wasted no time showing Lindy his latest acquisitions.

The roll of duct tape.

The rope.

And the knife.

He explained the true circumstances of his flight from his unmanageable life. He left nothing out. He was surprised by how readily she agreed to his proposition. "It's the only way," he said. "I'm tired of fighting it. I'm tired of everything."

When she had him secured to the bed, she said, "Don't act so surprised. I told you, baby—I'm a truth-seeker, too. But I'm the real deal. Not like you, you wimp. I don't flinch from truth."

Then she affixed the duct tape to his mouth and showed him her own knife.

A knife that was an exact replica of the one from his dreams.

No, he thought, *it really is the one from my dreams.*

This is the truth.

This is what I was always trying to see.

I dreamed the future in reverse.

When he felt the first slice of the knife, he felt a profound gratitude.

Melinda, a child abuse and rape victim with a long history

of mental illness, said, "Here's your truth, Kyle. I am the great avenger. I am the equalizer. I go here and I go there, hither and yon, and everywhere I go, I punish men for the sins of mankind."

But Kyle didn't care about her psychosis.

All that mattered to him was that his suffering was nearly at an end.

About that, though, he was mistaken.

She was very skilled, very practiced.

She worked on him for a long, long time, slicing him with her knife long past dawn. Then she took another shower and left him before the maid arrived. When the cleaning lady entered the room, she loosed a shrill scream that brought her fellow workers running.

Several people crowded into the room.

A desk clerk vomited.

A guest from the room across the hall said, "Oh, that poor man."

Somebody else said. "Christ, call 911, he's still alive."

When the duct tape was stripped from his face and the gag removed from his mouth, Kyle pleaded with them to kill him.

"He's delirious," somebody said.

"The pain's making him crazy."

"God, I hope the paramedics get here soon."

Kyle cried out in agony.

He pleaded with them some more.

And he went right on living.

While all these strangers kept gazing upon this hideous, nasty, ugly, inescapable truth.

His nightmare revealed.

LEFT FOR DEAD (MOON CHILD ASCENDING)

By the time the stolen Lexus swerved to the side of the dark back road, Mitch MacCaffrey was a broken man. Every ounce of false bravado was gone. He was done with the flippant remarks and the impotent, pseudo-tough guy threats. The barrel of Logan Caine's Glock pushed harder against his side.

Mitch screwed his eyes hut and waited for the explosion.

For that horrible moment of mind-bending agony.

He heard a door open, the front passenger door from the sound of it. Then a crunch of shoulder gravel beneath booted feet. The door to his right came open and he was yanked out of the car.

Logan Caine scrambled out after him.

So they wouldn't do it in the car. Of course they wouldn't. The Lexus wouldn't be a known stolen vehicle for some time, but they wouldn't want to drive around in a bloody mess of a car. Too conspicuous.

So Mitch had a reprieve.

Probably a very short one.

A few precious seconds, maybe. The notion that his time on earth was down to that terrified him. The unfairness of it was too much. He wasn't a bad guy. He'd made a few mistakes, errors in judgment, but he didn't deserve this.

Nobody should know this kind of terror.

This helplessness, this total, soul-baring emasculation.

Mitch opened his eyes are saw Derrick Mullins aiming the barrel of a Sig Sauer at his forehead. Mitch cringed and saw it happen in his mind, saw the muzzle spit fire and saw this bullet punch through his forehead and blow his brains out the back of his skull. Tears streamed down his cheeks and a snot bubble swelled out of one nostril and popped.

"Please…" His voice was horse, thick with sobs and desperation. "Please…don't kill me…I won't testify. I swear. You don't have to kill me."

Logan Caine laughed.

The fine-tuned engine of the Lexus revved. A window rolled down and Dal Higgins, the man behind the wheel, said, "Don't fuck around. Do it and let's get out of here."

Mitch squealed.

An embarrassing sound.

The sound a spoiled child makes when his favorite toy is taken away as punishment for misbehavior. He reached out with groping, pleading hands for the front of Logan Caine's guayabera. "Please…have mercy…I have a daughter…"

Logan groaned. "Aw, not that shit." He snorted laughter. "Christ, I hate it when they start in with that 'I've got a kid!' shit, like that's gonna help 'em."

Mitch managed to snag a handful of smooth fabric with one fumbling hand. "Please…"

Logan clubbed him upside the head with the Glock.

Mitch yelped and pitched sideways. He was off-balance and his arms pinwheeled wildly in a desperate effort to restore his equilibrium. But Derrick Mullins drove a booted foot hard into his stomache and sent him reeling into the ditch. The back of his head struck a rock and pain exploded in his head and arced down his body like forked lightning. His vision went away in a burst of white light.

When he could see again, he saw only darkness.

Then he saw the white crescent of a quarter-moon suspended high in the sky above him. For a moment, he forgot about his predicament, forgot he was about to die. He was overwhelmed by the loveliness of the rural sky at night. Jesus, you could actually see the stars out here. He lifted a shaky hand to the sky, reaching for the moon, imagining he could hook his fingers around one indented edge of that white sliver.

But the moment of mysticism passed.

He saw Logan Caine and Derrick Mullins looming over him. They looked like giants standing at the edge of the ditch. Cloaked in the shadow of the nearby forest, they looked like Satan's own foot soldiers, leering harbingers of doom.

The guns pointing down at him looked like hands of judgment.

He heard Logan Caine's guff voice one more time. "Say goodbye, Mitch."

The Glock and the Sig Sauer discharged several times. A bullet whizzed by Mitch's throat and embedded itself into the soft earth.

It was the only shot that missed.

A slug punctured his stomach. So did another, popping beer-gut flesh like a potato bag. The large caliber rounds punched all the way through him, creating holes in his lower back that pumped blood into the ground. Another bullet shattered a rib and lodged inside him. Two more entered the region just slightly north of his groin. The high-velocity invaders stung like bees, but that initial snap of pain was nothing compared to the wash of agony that engulfed him once his nerve-endings responded to the damage. There was little conscious thought at this point, just perfect awareness of total pain, but he did manage a prayer for a bullet to the head.

For an end to his suffering.

But the guns fell silent.

Logan Caine said, "That oughta do it."

Mitch wailed.

Derrick Mullins glanced at Logan. "He ain't dead. I'll put one in his head."

He raised his arm to aim again, but Logan gripped his wrist. "Nah, fuck it, man. He'll die in a few minutes." He chuckled. "Let the asshole get the full experience."

Mullins smiled. "Sure. Whatever."

They got back in the car and Dal Higgins stepped on the accelerator. The Lexus pulled away from the shoulder, then he heard the car gathering speed as it zoomed away from him. The engine noise swelled for another moment, then quickly receded.

They were gone.

Mitch McCaffrey's eyes filled with tears. He was all alone. He was going to die here in this ditch. Unnoticed. With nobody to comfort him as he slipped into the abyss—or stepped into the light, or whatever it was that really happened when you died. He thought of his father, who'd made it to eighty-two and had died in relative peace on a hospital bed. An image from that night taunted Mitch, the face of the friends and family gathered around the dying man's bed.

God, how he wanted someone with him now.

He was terrified of facing this alone.

He cried out for his mother.

Who was in a nursing home hundreds of miles away. Lois McCaffrey had advanced Alzheimer's and wouldn't recognize her youngest son if she saw him.

But there were other people who cared for him. Sally, his seven-year-old daughter. Karen, his ex-wife, with whom he'd still harbored hope for a reconciliation. No chance of that now. His siblings, Jeremy and Heather. Some of his closer friends and business associates. Yeah, there were still people who would mourn his passing. Despite the series of fuck-ups that had steered him toward this sorry end, people liked him.

What would those people make of the manner of his death?

No point contemplating that.

Mitch knew what they would think. That he'd brought it on himself. That it was what you got for doing business with people like Logan Caine's boss.

And they would be right.

Mitch blinked and again saw the crescent moon. It was so beautiful. There was something…spiritual about his perception of it now, a feeling totally removed from his internalized images of lunar landings and men in bulky spacesuits bouncing around a grey, rock-strewn landscape. He stared at it now, seeking to transcend the pain through a focus of will. He imagined his soul, his spirit, slipping free of its physical moorings and rising high above the earth, ascending not to heaven but toward the moon. He saw it in his mind, his essence rising skyward, glancing back to see his body getting smaller and smaller until it disappeared.

Until the earth itself became a floating globe below him.

He smiled at the sense of freedom he would have. He was gripped by a fervent wish that it really be this way. He prayed for his soul to be liberated from this ruined shell. He wanted to exist on that other plane, that place where spirits were free of human frailty and avarice, a place of perfect peace.

The mental diversion was lovely for a few moments, but the reality of his corporeal senses overwhelmed the vision. He felt the salty tang of blood at the back of his throat. He tilted his head sideways and a stream of blood spilled from the corner of his mouth. Pain lashed him like a bullwhip and he twitched in the ditch, crying out again for his mother.

Dear, sweet old Mom.

The lights are on, but nobody's home.

Mitch tried to laugh, but more blood rushed out of his mouth.

Christ, why wasn't he dead yet?

It occurred to him that with the proper medical care he might stand a chance of surviving the damage inflicted on him. A slim chance, sure, but a chance nonetheless. The bullets had missed his heart and his head. His lungs didn't seem to have been punctured, which, considering where most of the shots had been aimed, was nothing less than a miracle. It wasn't out of the realm of possibility that a good trauma team and a skilled surgeon could save him. He'd heard of other people surviving multiple gunshots, so he knew such things were possible.

He also knew that survival hinged on receiving immediate treatment. Which just didn't seem to be in the cards for him. He cursed those assholes for dumping him in the middle of nowhere. It might be a long time before another vehicle came along. Even if somebody came by, they wouldn't be likely to see him down here, anyway.

Maybe if he could crawl out to the road…lie there flat on the asphalt.

Somebody would have to stop.

He turned his head to look at the road. It was just a few feet away, no more than a dozen. But it might as well have been on the other side of the world. Pain wracked his body every time he tried to move.

So Mitch gave up.

He stayed there on his back and kept staring at the moon. Whatever marginal trace of a fighting spirit he'd managed to dredge up withered and died. He was again resigned to facing his end in this stinking ditch.

He cried some more.

Spit up some more blood.

He thought, *If only I could hurry up and die, if only I could kill myself somehow...*

If only I hadn't been so stupid.

After a while—it seemed like a long, *long* while—he began to feel lightheaded. The pain ebbed some. He was either losing consciousness or finally dying. He prayed for the latter. His vision blurred again, and the sliver of moon loomed large, magnified by the flood of moisture in his eyes. It bloomed like a brilliant flower, an explosion of beautiful light that obliterated everything else.

He didn't see the pale, dark-haired woman stepping out of the line of tree beyond the ditch.

The dizzy feeling became more pronounced.

This is it, he thought.

I'm almost dead.

Thank God.

The dark-haired woman knelt next to him in the ditch. Mitch became aware of a presence other than his own, and it brought him back from the brink for a moment. He blinked and saw the woman. When he saw how beautiful she was, how very much like an ethereal goddess of legend, he reached out to touch her cheek.

She smiled and kissed the back of his hand.

Then she gathered him in her arms and lifted him off the ground.

Mitch thought, This isn't real.

He was hallucinating, his ebbing consciousness filling his mind with dream-like visions of things that couldn't be. No woman, especially no woman as slender as this one, could life him with so little discernible effort.

But the vision persisted.

The woman carried him out of the ditch and into the forest. He was aware of low-hanging tree branches, the chirruping of crickets, and the occasional glimpse of lovely moonlight through the branches.

Oh, Mother, he thought again.

Oh, Mother moon...

Then, at last, the world faded to black.

Consciousness returned by degrees. His first awareness was tactile, a cool, smooth surface beneath his body. A warm fire crackled nearby. He rolled closer to the heat source, curled up in the fetal position, and slipped away again. He'd been too tired to register anything beyond the curious fact of his continued existence.

A while later, he awoke again.

He was in a small cave.

A fire burned in a pit a few feet away. He smelled food and a heavy scent of incense. The dark-haired woman sat cross-legged on the other side of the fire. The ankle-length dress he'd seen her wearing before was gone. She was nude, and the light from the fire bathed her body in a mellow, flickering light.

With a groan, Mitch sat up.

The woman smiled.

Mitch frowned. "Who are you?"

She tilted her head and something silver glittered beneath the hollow of her threat. Mitch squinted and leaned closer. His eyes widened when he saw the little silver crescent dangling from the delicate chain around her neck.

The moon, he thought.

The woman spoke. "I'm Diana."

The woman's rich, mellifluous voice was like nothing he'd ever head. It evoked so many feelings simultaneously. It was at once beautiful and forceful. It conveyed compassion and power. It was a lover's delicate whisper in his ear, and it was a stentorian, commanding *presence*.

It was an impossible voice.

Mitch wasn't sure what Diana was, but he knew she wasn't human.

He swallowed hard. "Why do I feel no pain?"

Her smile widened. "Because you belong to me now. You called me. You are a child of the moon."

"I called you?"

She rose gracefully to her feet. "Your spirit called me. You will serve me now."

She walked to the mouth of the cave, beckoning to Mitch with a curled forefinger. He got to his feet and followed her into the wild night.

A fat man was being tortured in an office of an abandoned warehouse. Handcuffed to a chair, he was bleeding from multiple straight-razor nicks to his bare torso. He was trying to talk to his tormentors, but what emerged from his mouth was reduced by sheer terror to nonsensical blubbering.

Logan Caine and Derrick Mullins paced about the room, their hard faces looking ominous in the harsh lantern light. Logan drew in a lungful of cigarette smoke, while Derrick twirled the straight-razor in his fingers.

Logan blew smoke in the fat man's face. "I don't think you're telling us everything, George."

"But I am!" A spray of spittle flew from the fat man's mouth. "Jesus, you guys know I'd never rat out Mr. Ligotti. I'm not that stupid."

Logan laughed. "Horseshit, George. You were stupid enough to wind up here, weren't you?"

He put his cigarette out on George's shoulder and laughed at his scream. He slapped the fat man twice to shut him up, seized a handful of his hair and yanked his head up. He leaned in close and said, "You talked, George. I know it. You know it. Derrick here knows it. And Mr. Ligotti sure as hell knows it. The feds hauled you in on a clean bust. You should be sitting in a cell right now. But you're not. Know what that tells me?"

George tried to talk but he'd become inarticulate again. "I-I-I…ooohh…"

Logan twisted the handful of hair, eliciting a yelp. "George, it tells me the feds scared your ass. They offered you a deal and you ran your mouth like a beauty salon gossip hag."

Derrick closed the straight-razor and put it away.

He produced the Sig Sauer from his shoulder holster. "I guess the feds didn't like you, Georgy Porgy. You oughta be in the WitSec program right now."

George blubbered some more.

Logan relinquished his hair and stepped away. "Fuck it. Cap the fat bastard so we can get out of here."

Derrick aimed the automatic pistol at the fat man's head.

Then the door to the office creaked open.

Mitch smiled at the identical thunderstruck expressions on the faces of his killers. Their mouths drooped open like those of kids at a magic show.

Mitch pulled the door shut. "Howdy, fellas. Glad to see me?"

Logan's voice emerged in a ragged whisper. "This shit ain't happenin'. You're dead, MacCaffrey."

Mitch looked at the man handcuffed to the chair. "Hey there, George."

The fat man's wide eyes glistened with tears. "Jesus…they told me you were dead, buddy."

Mitch began undoing the buttons of his shirt. "They were right, George." His gaze went back to Vincent Ligotti's thugs. "You guys wanna see something cool?"

Derrick shot a nervous glance at Logan. "I don't like this."

Logan Caine never looked away from Mitch. He pulled out his Glock and jacked a round into the chamber. He aimed the gun at the phantom's head. "Lock and load, Mullins. Let's do it right this time. Head shots."

Mitch tugged the shirt-tail out of his trousers.

Derrick's hand shook as he raised the Sig Sauer. Sweat streamed from his scalp and got in his eyes. He palmed the moisture away and glanced again at Logan. "Logan…"

"Derrick—"

Derrick took a step backward. "I really don't like this, man. Asshole shouldn't be up walking around, even if somebody saved his ass." He moved backward a few more steps, yelping when he collided with a desk. "Something's fucked-up here…"

Mitch shrugged the shirt off and let it fall to the floor. He smiled again. The ragged holes where the bullets had punctured his flesh were still there. He raised his hands high over his head like a ballerina and twirled slowly around so they could see the gaping exit wounds on his back. When he stood facing them again, he probed one of the wounds in his abdomen with an index finger.

Derrick Mullins shrieked.

Even the normally unflappable Logan Caine looked rattled. His jutting lower lip trembled and the hand holding the Glock began to shake. He grimaced when Mitch pushed the finger through the wound up to his top knuckle. When the walking dead man appeared to wiggle the finger inside him, Logan's stomach convulsed.

He choked back bile.

Mitch pulled the finger out. It glistened with an oily substance that might have been blood or some other bodily substance. Still smiling, Mitch stuck the finger in his mouth and slowly tongued off the viscous fluid.

Derrick's Sig Sauer fell from his fingers and clattered on the floor. He bent over, braced his hands on his knees, and spewed his pasta lunch all over George's blood-stained trousers.

Mitch laughed.

He stepped forward.

Logan's breath came out in a pant. Mitch could almost hear the jackhammer rhythm of his terror-juiced heart. "St-st-stay where you are, McCaffrey!"

He took a step back.

Mitch continued to advance, but he appeared to be in no hurry. "The most incredible thing happened when you guys left me to die in that ditch. I met a goddess. A real, honest-to-gosh *goddess*. Yeah, I know it sounds nuts. I know you don't believe me. But think about it guys." His grin broadened a little more. "It it any more far-fetched than the idea of a reanimated corpse returning to take revenge on his murderers?"

Logan Caine's trigger finger twitched.

A bullet punched through Mitch's shoulder.

Mitch barely flinched.

A moment later, he seized Logan's gun hand, pried the

Glock loose, and tossed it away. "You won't be needing that anymore, Logan."

He gripped Logan by the throat with one hand and ripped open the thug's guayabera with the other. Logan's exposed torso was shiny with sweat. The outstretched fingers of Mitch's right hand pushed through the soft flesh of the doomed criminal's abdomen with astonishing ease. Logan screamed and spasmed as Mitch pulled out a long coil of intestine. Mitch wrapped the length of wet, steaming viscera around Logan's throat, then he punched through the dying man's chest cavity and yanked out his still-beating heart.

There was an explosion in the room.

George screamed.

Mitch relinquished his hold on Logan and saw that Derrick Mullins had recovered his Sig Sauer. Logan tumbled dead to the floor. Mullins was slumped against a blood-spattered wall, the barrel of the gun protruding from his mouth.

Mitch's smile faded. "Coward."

He felt cheated.

He snapped the handcuffs off George's wrists, picked up his shirt, and departed without another word.

Mitch felt a sense of exhilaration as he drove through the city streets. He repeatedly reviewed the images from the warehouse office, savoring especially the way smug Logan Caine had lost his cool.

He felt all-powerful.

Like a god.

Was that what he was now? It didn't seem out of the realm of possibility. Hell, *nothing* seemed out of the realm of possibility anymore. The moon woman's strange magic had allowed him to continue existing on the physical plane even though he was dead. It had invested him with unnatural strength.

There's no limit to what I can do now, he thought.

I can go after Mr. Ligotti next. Hell, I can take over his organization. I can run this city's underworld myself and make more money than I ever dreamed of making.

The prospect was intoxicating.

No longer would he have to listen to the self-righteous diatribes of people who didn't want him to succeed. He realized his first order of business would be a visit to Karen. He'd set her right real good, make her see how fundamentally things had changed, and his family would be together again.

Mitch felt invincible.

Then he glanced in the rearview mirror and saw Diana sitting in the back.

He gasped. "Diana! What…what are you doing here?"

She smiled. "You have closed the circle. It is time for you to leave this world."

A sense of panic engulfed Mitch. His heart would have been thumping hard had he still been alive. "No. No. Fuck no." He looked at her again, shuddered at the power in those luminous eyes. "I don't wanna go. You don't understand. All my life I've wanted success and respect. Now I can have those things. Please don't make me give that chance up. It's not fucking fair."

Diana just kept smiling at him.

Mitch pulled the stolen car to the curb. There was no conscious decision to do this. Despairing, he realized he was through making decisions for himself. He got out of the car and stood in the middle of the street.

Diana appeared next to him.

She took his hand.

Mitch cringed as a tow-truck bore down on them.

The rumbling vehicle passed through them. Mitch realized his body lacked the solidity of just a few moments before. He was only incorporeal essence now. The magic granting his spirit physical form and substance had deserted him.

Diana smiled. "We're going home now, Moon Child."

He rose into the sky with Diana.

They rose high above the earth and the moon loomed large.

Home.

Where he would worship Diana and be a servant of the night forever.

Mitch experienced one more moment of longing, a desperate need to hold on to his earthly ambitions and appetites.

Then he surrendered and embraced the eternal night.

WALK AMONG US

1.
The Blood of Innocents

Jack Grimm stood at the edge of the sea and smoked a single Lucky Strike down to the filter. Cool water rolled up the beach and over his bare feet. The water receded. The tranquil rhythm of the tide might have been soothing under saner circumstances, but in Jack's line of work sane circumstances were rare.

Somewhere behind him lay the decomposing body of a five-hundred-year-old vampire. The sun was coming up fast, but the old vamp hadn't been vanquished by the dawning of the new day. Nope. Victor Heinritz, the self-styled "Lord of the Dark" (a name that made Jack roll his eyes every time he thought of it), had instead met his fate at the hands of the American South's premier private investigator specializing in crimes involving elements of the supernatural or otherworldly. Specifically, via a stake plunged straight through the middle of his stinking black heart by Jack Grimm.

Jack blew out a stream of smoke and glimpsed the still-wet blood of Count Jerkwad staining his fingers. He flipped the smoked-down filter into the ocean and knelt to wash the gore from his flesh. The blood stained the clear water, a cloud of drifting taint that rolled away from him a melancholy moment later. Jack sat there on his haunches a few moments longer, the cuffs of his grey trousers rolled up to his kness, thinking of all the other blood on his hands, stains no longer visible but that had left indelible marks on his soul. He thought of Mona, the long lost love who'd betrayed him so completely. He thought of his father, still alive but trapped somewhere in Hell. And he thought of all the people he'd failed through the years. People who had died, and people who were little more than empty husks waiting to die. He was so immersed in this dark turn of thought that he didn't hear the faint electric sizzle of the portal opening behind him.

Someone stepped through the portal and cleared his throat.

Jack blinked. He shook the water off his hands and stood up, turning around to see Andy O'Day striding toward him with the familiar silver flash of whiskey in one hand and a filled-to-the-brim pint glass of Guinness in the other.

Jack accepted the glass of Guinness and drank deeply of stout while Andy screwed the cap off the flask and imbibed from its bottomless depths. Literally bottomless. The flask never emptied of Irish whiskey. *It was a magic thing*, Andy was fond of saying, *you wouldn't understand.*

Andy's lean, tall form stood framed against the blazing circle of the portal, which crackled in the air a few feet above the ground, a magical wound in the flesh of the world. He capped the flask and returned it to an inner pocket of his leather jacket, then extracted a fresh pack of Lucky Strikes from another pocket. Marlboro was Andy's usual brand. Jack appreciated the gesture. Andy wedged a smoke into a corner of his thin-lipped mouth before proffering the pack to Jack. Jack accepted the pack, shaking out a cigarette he lit with his Zippo.

Andy exhaled smoke. "So…how did the big showdown with the dork lord go?"

Jack shrugged. "Went down the way I figured it. Vicky couldn't resist the scent of virgin blood. I stripped and waited in the water while Lucy played bait on the beach. Poor son of a bitch never knew what hit him, he was so entranced by his succulent prize."

Andy nodded and exhaled more smoke. "And Lucy?"

Jack's expression darkened and he turned his gaze to the horizon. "She survived, but he got his fangs in her."

"I see." Andy's tone was neutral, but Jack thought he

detected a hidden note of reproach. "Will she turn?"

"I don't know." He sighed. "I guess I ought to stay another day, see what happens."

Andy shook his head. "No can do, mate."

Jack's frown deepened and he turned to look his old friend and half-brother in the eye again. "Excuse me? It's my fault she's in this mess. If she turns—"

Andy jabbed an index finger in Jack's direction. "If she turns, she turns. It'll be too bad, but she knew what she was doing. That bastard wiped out her whole family. And God knows how many thousands of others through the ages. She knew the risk of being killed or turned was high."

Jack's brow furrowed as raw anger flowed into his veins like a fast-acting poison. "Which is exactly why we can't allow her to become what he was."

Andy shook his head. "I understand how you feel, but you did what you came here to do, Jack. What Lucy paid you to do. There's more pressing business to see to back home."

Jack closed his eyes. He could feel the onset of a wicked headache flaring to life behind his eyes. "What now?"

Andy chuckled. "You won't believe it."

Jack's eyes fluttered open. He scowled. "I've killed vampires, werewolves, and demons. I've been to Hell and made it back alive. So you'll have to forgive me if I doubt your word, ol' buddy. Tell me what I won't believe."

Andy smirked. "One word, Jack. Want to guess what that word is?"

"I don't feel up to guessing games, Andy."

"You're no fun when you're in one of your angsty moods, Jackie." Andy took another deep drag from his cigarette and flicked it away. "The word, Jack, is aliens. And I'm not talking about illegal immigrants. I'm taking about capital-V Visitors. Extraterrestrials. Beings not of this world."

"I get the picture." Jack studied Andy's expressions, which had turned suddenly sober. "You're serious?"

"I knew you wouldn't believe it."

Jack grunted. "Oh, I believe it."

Andy frowned. "Seriously? Damn. I was hoping I'd

finally come up with something that'd have you absolutely flabbergasted."

A corner of Jack's mouth twitched, a near smirk. Andy was having a bit of fun with him. His brother often knew things Jack did not, including a deep wealth of things most people would never guess. "Yeah, I already knew about this. But why the urgency? I thought they were peaceful?"

"That's a mistaken impression, Jack. They're really quite nasty. And they have plans, Jack. They've been staking out territory, setting up operations, getting up to all sorts of nefarious shenanigans. They've got to be stopped. Now."

Jack shrugged. "Wouldn't this be a matter for the government, then?"

Andy laughed heartily.

In a moment Jack was laughing just as hard. He managed to compose himself long enough to say, "Good point."

Andy nodded. "Let's get cracking then, eh?"

Jack sighed again. "Sure, why not?"

They stepped through the blazing portal, which immediately ceased to exist, leaving the rapidly decaying carcass of Victor Heinritz alone on that windy stretch of bone-white beach.

2.
Trouble On The Way

Jack Grimm stepped out of the portal and into the stock room of the Sherlock Holmes Pub in Nashville. Andy was ahead of him, already moving toward the door to the bar. The door opened and Andy moved through a vertical rectangle of light. Sounds from the bar filtered into the stock room, laughter, boisterous conversation, Celtic music, and the faint tinkling of glassware.

Jack thought, *Not again.*

On rare occasions a trip through a magic portal took them through a gap in time. The gaps were usually quite short, anywhere from a matter of a few minutes to as much as a day or so. This time looked to be toward the longer end of that spectrum. Jack suspected they'd lost nearly an entire day. But the occasional small time gaps were the least disconcerting aspect of portal travel. Actually stepping through one of Andy's portals was the hard part. All awareness vanished upon entering that blackness. It was like ceasing to exist for a time, like an atheist's concept of what death must be like. Spooky as hell, in other words. Portal travel was a necessary evil in their line of work, but Jack hated it. He hoped like hell the jump ahead in the time stream wouldn't come back to haunt them this time, but Jack figured it probably would. His luck ran that way. If there was any possibility things could go bad—really, *REALLY* bad—then they probably would. He recalled the sense of urgency in Andy's tone during his quick summary of the alien problem and shuddered.

Sweet Jesus, he thought, *What am I stepping into here?*

Jack moved through the open door and immediately caught sight of several familiar faces arrayed around the bar and sitting in rickety chairs at a handful of wooden tables. Many of them acknowledged him with a nod and a grin. A few pretended not to see him. One such person in the latter category—a tall, strikingly handsome man with long black hair—slid off his barstool and followed them out of the bar.

Jack and Andy waited for Lucien on the sidewalk outside the pub. By the time the hellhound joined them, Jack had already smoked another Lucky Strike halfway to the filter.

The pub's front door swung open and Lucien stepped outside. He declined Jack's offer of a cigarette with a shake of his head that caused the long hair to fall across his face. He brushed the hair back and said, "They're coming."

Jack gave a barely perceptible nod. "Now, right?"

The fierceness of Lucien's gaze made the answer clear.

Jack said, "From where?"

Lucien's lips barely moved as he said, "From everywhere. Behind you. From the pub. To our left. To our right. We have maybe a few seconds."

Jack looked at Andy. His half-brother's eyes communicated a decision that didn't need to be verbalized. Jack detected movement in his peripheral vision, the pub's front door opening again. Light glinted off something metallic. Jack's cigarette slipped from his fingers and tumbled end over flaming end to the sidewalk as his hand moved in a flash to the .45 in his shoulder holster. The gun was in his hands and aimed at the pub's door less than a heartbeat later. Andy O'Day produced his weapon just as quickly and aimed at something behind Jack. For one breathless, frozen moment the world seemed to stand absolutely still.

Then Jack's forefinger squeezed the trigger of the .45. The big caliber gun made a big sound

BLAM!

and sent a bullet zipping through the air. The round struck the forehead of a big, burly, bearded man clad in leather, punching a neat hole all the way through where his brain should have been—but there was no rain of blood and brain matter against the pub door, nor did any leak from the forehead hole. Jack kept firing even as Andy's own weapon started to erupt. Spent shell casings rained on the sidewalk.

PLINKPLINKPLINKLPLINK

and glittered in the streetlight before rolling off the curb into the storm drain. The faux-biker's body was soon riddled with holes and it fell back against the bar's entrance. It was shaken, but far from out of the game. It looked at Jack and grinned as it struggled to push away from the door. There was no more doubt the grinning jackass was an alien. A real human would be dead already, flat on his back, bleeding out on the ground. A primal fear rose in Jack, but he dropped a psychical equivalent of a manhole-sized lid on top of it, shutting it deep down into the recesses of his brain. There was no time for fear in a situation like this, no time to wonder how in hell you might kill something that gave every appearance of being unkillable.

So he squeezed the .45's trigger until it clicked empty. He ejected the spent cartridge even as Andy spun on his heel, drew a bead on something to their right, and kept firing. Jack calmly stood his ground as the alien at last managed to push away from the door and come lurching toward him. He slammed a fresh cartridge into the .45 with the base of a fist and drew down on the biker alien again.

Before he could start firing again, the air next to him shimmered and grew warm as Lucien shapeshifted. A savage growl reverberated in the street and saliva from the hellhound's snarling mouth hit the sidewalk and sizzled, the corrosive fluid eating through concrete as easily as a stream of lava burning through timber. Another stuttering growl rang out, then Lucien sprang at something outside Jack's field of vision. There was a heavy thud as the hellhound drove the body of an alien to the ground, followed by the agonized wail of the alien.

The sound of the thing's pain heartened Jack. It meant they could be hurt. Maybe even killed—at least by a supernaturally powerful refugee from Hell. Jack directed some more high velocity lead at the biker alien, obliterating most of its head with a tightly centered series of blasts to its face. The thing tottered sideways a moment, swayed on its feet, then feel to the ground in a unmoving heap. Jack kept his gaze on the downed alien a moment longer, not quite trusting the reality of its death, then he released a breath he hadn't realized he'd been holding and glanced around him, taking quick stock of the situation.

Lucien, still in full-hound mode, looked up at him from the sidewalk, his muzzle flecked with bit of shredded flesh—but no blood. Instead, the insides of these things were filled with a vaguely ectoplasmic white goo that stank worse than a chest-high pile of manure.

Andy, who'd guessed the proper kill method sooner, had dropped three of the things. Their faceless, nearly headless bodies lay still in the street and on the sidewalk, leaking goo on concrete and asphalt.

Jack's heart pounded.

Awareness of the rest of the world hit him with the force of a cannonball to the head. His first thoughts were of damage control and of how to escape. The police would be here within moments, and there'd be no way to explain any of this in a way that'd make sense to normal people. His gaze swept the street. He saw people cowering in doorways and behind parked cars lining both sides of the street.

Jack laughed. It was desperate laughter. His own office was on this side of the street, just a couple of buildings down to the left. But there would be no sanctuary there tonight. Not after a big-time Technicolor shootout in the middle of a crowded city street.

Lucien's hound form shimmered and he resumed his human form, his tattered clothes hanging from him like rags, making him look like a wolfman from some old movie. Jack met his gaze, nodded, then looked at Andy.

"You thinking what I'm thinking?"

Andy put his gun away, palmed his pack of Lucky Stikes from his jacket pocket and calmly lit a smoke. Andy liked to project an air of absolutely imperturbable cool. He wanted you to think he was the coolest, smoothest, calmest dude in the world. At times like this, Jack suspected he was exactly that.

Andy exhaled a stream of smoke, cleared his throat. "Yeah, mate. Let's portalize our asses outta here."

Using the tip of the cigarette, he described a circle in the air as he intoned a series of Latin phrases. The circle shimmered. It was more of an oval, really, Jack thought. Then there was a black, fire-ringed space in the fabric of reality.

Andy, puffing on his cigarette again, stepped through it.

Jack and Lucien, careful to keep their feet away from the flickering flames, followed.

3.
Another Random Hell

The sun was a burning orb hanging high in the sky, projecting intense heat that felt absolutely unfiltered. *Ozone layer*, Jack thought deliriously. *What goddamned ozone layer?*

"So any idea where we are?"

Andy chuckled. "The desert."

Jack sneered. "You know what, Andy? Believe it or not, I'm not in the mood for sarcasm. I know this is a desert. So I'll clarify. *Which* goddamn desert?"

Andy shrugged. "Dunno. Looks familiar, though."

Lucien groaned. "No. It can't be."

Jack shook his head and sighed. "Nevada. Again. Christ."

"Makes sense," Andy said, nodding as he stripped off his shiny blue button-down shirt, exposing flesh so pale Jack figured the guy would be bright red within minutes.

Jack's own flesh was only marginally darker, so he resisted

the urge to shed some of his own garments. The heat was suffocating, but he figured he could endure that better than becoming one big man-sized sunburn. Bad enough that he'd left his wingtips on that Florida beach. The desert sand beneath his feet was blisteringly hot. The heat was so oppressive he didn't even feel like lighting a cigarette.

Lucien, though, didn't appear too bothered by the heat. It figured. A hellhound wouldn't be too adversely affected by conditions such as these.

Lucky son of a bitch.

Jack directed a smirk Andy's way. "You might want to work up some SPF 50 mojo, bro. Unless you want to wind up a crispy red blotch on the desert floor."

Andy winked. "Already taken care of."

Jack rolled his eyes. "Freaking wizard. Always one step ahead, eh? And by the way, why in the hell does being back in Nevada make sense?"

Andy lit a cigarette.

Jack glared at him.

Andy snickered. "Ah, well. It's like this, Jackie. Any time I have to work out mystical coordinates on the fly like that, when time is really of the essence, I have to make some shortcuts, let the portal take us back to a previous destination."

Jack frowned. "And you let it take us *here*? You're aware Satan's minions are everywhere here, right?"

"Everywhere, eh?" Andy made an exaggerated show of scanning the wide-open desert landscape around them. "Huh. They must be invisible."

Jack snarled and ripped the pack of cigarettes from Andy's hand. "Oh, screw you. Think you're funny, huh?"

"Sometimes. And for your information, no, I didn't pick this destination." Andy hesitated. An almost sheepish look stole over his handsome features. It was an odd sight. Andy almost never seemed abashed about anything. "It sort of…well, on the fly like that, as I was saying…um…it sort of happens at random."

Jack's jaw dropped. His stomach did a slow, wrenching churn. He tried to say something, but the right words momentarily eluded him.

Lucien supplied them: "We could be in Greytown right now."

Jack gulped. Greytown was a section of Hell. A sort of outlying suburb that resembled New Jersey more than any fire and brimstone preacher's lake of fire visions of that netherworld. It was where he'd met Lucien.

That moment of awe and absolute terror passed. Anger took its place. "Andy, I give you a lot of crap, I know, but you know I've got great faith in you. You've gotten us out of a lot of tight jams. But dammit, man, you know how screwed we'd be, hell, how screwed the whole world would be, if we wound up back in Greytown."

Andy sighed. "I know. Okay? But we're not in Hell. Things worked out."

Lucien snorted. "Right. We're in the desert. Near the earthly home base of our most serious adversary." He shook his head, making long, sweat-drenched black locks flop about his shoulders. "We should've just run for it."

Jack nodded. "Damn right."

Andy heaved an exasperated sigh. "I get the point, okay? I screwed up but what's done is done. Hindsight's 20/20, all that jazz. In a minute, I'll do a more precise portal spell and get us the hell out of here. But before we jump back into the fray home, let's take a moment to take stock of things."

Jack shook a cigarette out of the pack and lit it, unable to resist the impulse of deep addiction any longer. "Fine. Advise us, oh wise one."

Andy nodded. The old fire came into his eyes again and he spoke with his usual authoritative confidence. "Here's the lowdown on the aliens. They're not invaders. They're not part of an advance guard paving the way for the colonization of earth by legions of little green bastards. They're rogues. Criminals. A gang. Think of them as being like the first New York mobsters who entered Florida way back when. That's what they're doing in Nashville. Establishing a base of operations."

Jack drew in a lungful of sweet, bracing smoke, then slowly expelled it. "Okay. Which better explain why it's not a job for the government. Hell, for all we know the local gov's taking kickbacks from these guys." He frowned. "So…er…what exactly sort of crimes are these Plan 9 mafiosos into anyway?"

Andy's expression grew grim. "Lots of the usual. Racketeering. Prostitution. Stuff we wouldn't even bother with under normal circumstances."

Lucien abruptly cocked his head and turned away from them. He moved several feet to the east and raised a hand to his brow, squinting against the blazing sun and refracted light on the horizon. "Um…guys?"

Jack said, "I'm assuming there's something else at work here, right? Something unusual?"

Andy flicked his spent cigarette butt away. "We're talking about human slavery, Jack. These extraterrestrial sons of bitches are snatching people and shipping them back to paying customers light years away from here."

Jack gave a moment's thought to what sadistic aliens might do with their human slaves and felt a fresh surge of molten anger. "You're right. We've got to stop them."

Lucien's voice came louder this time: "Shut up! Something's coming."

The urgency in the hellhound's voice at last drew the attention of his comrades. Jack and Andy abruptly dropped further discussion of the alien dilemma and moved to where Lucien was standing. They each mimicked his hand-to-brow stance and squinted at the hazy horizon.

Jack gulped.

Lucien was right. Something was coming. Multiple somethings, in face. Black specks hurtling across the desert from several directions at once, all of them apparently intent on converging on one spot.

THIS spot, Jack thought glumly.

"Um…hey, Andy…"

"Working on it already, mate."

Jacked looked at his half-brother. He'd quickly shrugged back into his jacket and shiny blue shirt, which hung open over his pale torso. He moved several feet away from Jack and Lucien, closed his eyes, and, with great deliberation, began to intone the pertinent Latin phrases. Jack frowned. Andy normally didn't close his eyes for this. He was likely working to blot out the fast-approaching danger and focus on the spell, hoping, Jack guessed, to avoid a repeat of the random portal debarkation debacle.

Andy's lips continued to move, the arcane phrases emerging quietly from his mouth, weaving an aura of magic layer by careful mystical layer. Jack appreciated the effort, but he was tempted to urge the wizard to a quick finish. They'd just have to take their chances, because if they weren't zipping through interdimensional space within a matter of moments they'd either be dead or on their way back to Hell alive.

Dead would be better. Jack knew this from experience.

In Jack's case, he was destined to arrive in Hell eventually. He was one of the Damned. Just one of the very many unsettling things he'd learned during his time there. But he'd like to delay his return to the infernal realm as long as possible. This, perhaps, being the most cosmic understatement he could imagine. Long enough to maybe redeem his tarnished soul and avoid it altogether. There were a few things of which Jack was absolutely certain and this was one of them—that redemption had not yet occurred.

Jack's gaze flickered rapidly back and forth from Andy to the oncoming hordes. They were close enough now that he could hear the buzz of engines, coming at them on black jeeps and motorcycles. A few of the former looked to have military-issue machine guns mounted in the rear. The men manning the weapons wore black masks and big, glassy goggles. They looked like they should be hounding Mel Gibson on a post-apocalyptic Australian landscape. Jack didn't bother reaching for his .45, nor did Lucien shift to hound mode. There was no point, no way they could hope to defend themselves against such overwhelming odds.

Andy's lips were still moving. Jack couldn't hear the Latin words anymore. They buzz of the engines had become a low roar. Jack's breathing quickened and his heart thummed like the plucked string of an electric guitar. The air nearby grew hotter as the outline of a portal began to take shape a foot above the desert floor. It was an oval ring of faint light with a grayish center. Andy's lips moved faster and the center darkened. But it wasn't happening fast enough.

One of the machine guns began to chug, spitting shell casings high into the bright desert sky. The shooter was still too far away, but Jack figured that would only remain the case for perhaps another thirty seconds. *If* they were lucky.

The portal's center was now as black as the heart of darkness itself. The ring of light surrounding it intensified and abruptly gave way to dancing flames.

More machine guns opened fire. The desert floor seemed to vibrate as the dozen of speeding vehicles bore relentlessly down on them.

And still Andy's lips moved.

Jack made a decision. "Oh, fuck this."

Lucien said, "I second that emotion."

They each grabbed Andy by an arm and dragged him toward the portal. Andy didn't resist, but his mouth kept working, strengthening and refining the delicate spell with each precious remaining second. Jack could hear the Latin phrases now. As always, it sounded like gibberish to him. But, he hoped, effective gibberish. The wizard was still working his mojo when Jack and Lucien tossed him through the portal.

Lucien glanced at Jack and stepped in after him.

Jack started to follow, but a mad impulse made him hesitate. A defiant spark of pissed-off attitude from his self-destructive side. He turned to the approaching onslaught of Satan's minions, raised both hands high into the air, and showed them two proudly raised middle fingers.

A machine gun bullet whined by his head.

Another nicked the sagging sleeve of his blazer.

Jack at last surrendered to common sense and dove through the portal.

4.
Hail, Hail, The Gang's All Here

He landed painfully on the hardwood floor of his Elliston Place office in Nashville. Several machine gun bullets passed through the portal an instant before it closed, punching a zig-zag pattern of holes through the wall separating the outer reception area from Jack's actual office.

The portal closed with a whooshing rush of air, the space it occupied sizzling and glimmering for a moment before returning to normal. Jack got to his hands and knees with a groan and heaved a big breath.

He heard Andy's voice first. "You all right, mate?"

Jack looked up. "No. I'm about as far from all right as I can be and still be drawing breath. How the hell did that happen? How did they find out we were there so quickly and get so many of their people after us within minutes?"

Lucien extended a hand to Jack and helped the weary detective to his feet. "You know why, Jack. That place is the center of their power in your world. We were lucky not to be squished like bugs the moment we landed in the desert. They've obviously been maintaining a vigil ever since we took down their old Vegas headquarters last year, hoping we'd be stupid enough to one day wonder back into their territory and give them another shot at us."

Jack chuckled in a dry, humorless way. "Which is just what we did." His gaze went to Andy. "But I've got to applaud you this time, brother. You did good. Nearly got us killed from taking so long, but that's beside the point."

Andy acknowledged the compliment with a nod. He took out his flask and spun the cap off, drinking deeply before passing it to Jack. Jack took a quick nip and passed it to Lucien. Andy waited until the flask was back in his hands before speaking. "Okay, we're back. We've had a series of close calls, and while it's tempting to take a bit of a break, bitter reality won't allow us that relief. It's time to deal with the aliens."

Jack started to say something, but the words died at the tip of his tongue, quashed by the sound of a key turning in the front lock. Lucien growled, and Jack and Andy went for their guns.

Then the door swung open, admitting Raven Rainbolt and the ghost of Harlan Calhoun. Raven didn't flinch at the sight of the guns pointed in her direction. She smirked and said, "Hi, guys. Where have you been keeping yourselves lately?" She bustled past them and made a show of wrinkling her nose at the scent of whiskey on their breaths. "Harlan and I have been busy, seeing new clients, doing some actual investigating. Basically keeping the business afloat while you guys stay out partying."

The slim, diminutive black-haired girl moved behind the reception desk and plopped into her usual seat. She glanced at the bullet holes in the wall behind her and smirked again. "Been shooting off your popguns indoors again?"

Andy cleared his throat. "Listen, missy—"

Jack cut him off. "It's not like that. We just had a narrow escape."

Raven arched an eyebrow. "Oh?"

Jack nodded. "A series of them, actually." He sighed. "I'd give you a rundown of events, but we're in an emergency situation here, one of those 'time is of the essence' kinda deals."

Raven laughed and shook her head. "Let me guess. The fate of the world rests in our hands. Again."

Jack frowned. "Well…not quite the 'world'…such as."

Now it was Raven's turn to frown. She looked at Andy. "Mr. O'Day, does this have anything to do with the situation we were discussing last week?

Andy said, "Yes. Probably. Maybe. That was, er…yesterday. I thought."

Raven pursed her lips and regarded him the way one regards a raving lunatic. She, like the rest of them, was used to Andy O'Day's often eccentric behavior, which included his tendency to show up when you least expected him to, his frequent and wildly inappropriate conversational non sequiturs, and the uncanny way he was nearly always several steps ahead of everyone else, regardless of the situation. Andy O'Day, as Jack so succinctly put it on more than one occasion, could freak you right the hell out. This time, however, Raven's expression indicated a certainty that he'd at last thoroughly lost his mind.

She shook her head slowly—her eyes narrowed to a suspicious squint—and said, "Noooo. That was last week. The alien thing, right?"

Andy nodded. "Ah. A-ha. Well…yes, the alien thing."

"Good." Raven smiled brightly. "That was definitely last week, then. I remember it clearly. It was the day before Jack's showdown with Heinrich."

Jack, Lucien, and Andy all exchanged nervous looks.

Jack coughed. "Say, Raven…what's today's date?"

Raven glanced at her desktop Onion calendar. "The 28th of May."

"Whoa." Andy whistled. "That's one hell of a time gap."

Jack scowled at Andy. "That's six days, Andy. Six… fucking…DAYS!"

Andy shrugged. "To be fair, you didn't let me finish my incantations."

"That's because we were about to be perforated by a hail of high-caliber bullets."

"A technicality."

The ghost of Harlan Calhoun chuckled and appeared to walk through the reception desk. He sat in a chair next to Raven, folded his arms, and said, "You ever think how much duller things would be without these guys in your life?"

A smile twitched at the corners of Raven's delicate mouth, but she suppressed the expression. "Mostly I think of how nice a normal life would be. You know, living in the suburbs, having a family, raising 2.5 kids, going to church on Sunday." Her tone became one of mock reverence and wonder. "The American Dream."

Jack rolled his eyes. "You're as normal as I am sober." The comment elicited a round of general laughter, which Jack acknowledged with an annoyed, impatient wave of the hand. "Okay, so technically we've been out of action for a week. I assume you've been following up on whatever it was you discussed with my spell-mangling brother last week."

"Indeed I have."

"Elucidate, please.'"

Lucien grunted. "'Elucidate.' What's that? Your vocabulary word for the day?

Jack's gaze remained on the girl as he raised a middle finger in Lucien's direction. "Well, Raven?"

Raven sat up straighter in her chair and wheeled closer to the desk. Her hands went to the keyboard in front of the flat-screen monitor and rapidly tapped some keys. After a pause, she tapped some more keys, studied what was on the screen a moment longer, then leaned back in her chair with a sigh and looked at the men.

She clasped her hands in front of her, steepling the forefingers in a way that made her look like an intensely focused young professor examining a complex equation scrawled across a chalkboard. If Andy was the mystic guiding spirit behind the Grimm Detective Agency, then Raven was the brains of the operation.

And what am I? Jack wondered.

But he knew the answer to that question. Much as he was loathe to admit it, he knew he wasn't quite the intellectual equal of Andy or Raven, or even Lucien. His function, beyond being the agency's namesake, existed at a much more primal level. He was the guts of GDA. Its beating heart and its tattered, but resilient soul. The other guys were no slouches when it came to facing danger, but everyone knew Jack was the go-to guy for getting in the faces of the bad guys. And he had a strong hunch he was about to be called upon to play that pivotal role yet again.

Raven's dark eyes locked on his own. He saw a spark of something there that had nothing to do with the current investigation. There was a chemistry between them strong enough to make Jack's breath catch in his throat in moments like this. The attraction had never been acted upon by either of them, not even in the vaguest way, but the erotic potential was a tangible thing.

Raven said, "Andy and Lucien did a good bit of digging into this matter while you were in Florida." She smiled slightly. "They were perhaps less subtle with their inquiries than usual. It's the reason the bad guys were able to spring that trap on you at the pub last week."

Andy made an exasperated sound. "Here we go with the blame game again."

Raven shook her head. "No, we're long past that. They were homing in on us. They knew that we knew their secrets. An attempted ambush would've happened regardless of our actions from that point." Her gaze settled on Jack again. "I have a job for you, Jack."

Jack straightened his tie and nodded. "I figured."

5.
A Stunning Reversal

Jack had been telling Andy the truth on that Florida beach. He'd known of the presence of aliens in Nashville for some time. Allusions to them had come up from time to time over the course of various investigations through the years. These usually occurred in the course of interrogating assorted stooges and minor-league bad guys, most of whom were looking to trade any random scrap of info to avoid being either turned over to the police or having to face another mouthful of Jack Grimm's brass knuckles. Most of the time, these minor leaguers weren't very smart. They didn't realize how infinitely more likely the latter was than the former.

Jack and the NPD didn't get along. Well…that was the nice way of putting it. They hated each other's guts was Jack's preferred bullshit-free way of putting it.

Over time, though, Jack became intrigued enough by these wildly swirling underworld rumors of Visitors to do a little off-duty digging on the subject. Despite some initial resistance among the small local Visitor community Jack soon learned the rumors were true. He ruffled enough alien feathers to warrant a visit from a representative of the community, an individual who claimed to be the highest-ranking authority among the several dozen or so members of his people living in the area.

The alien's true name was something Jack figured he could only pronounce if some brand of radical and horrendous surgery was performed on his vocal chords. The human name he used was Bill. Bill looked like a very average white man in his mid-forties, with short, receding brown hair going to gray, a slight beer paunch, and little tufts of wild hairs growing out of his ears and nostrils. He wore wire-rimmed bifocals, khaki slacks, loafers, and a not-very-stylish button-down shirt with a blue-and-yellow checkered pattern.

He looked a lot like Jack's late uncle, Patrick Grimm.

However, as Bill revealed to Jack during their conversation, the bland human appearance was only a masquerade. The aliens had the ability to craft humanoid constructs in which they could comfortably exist during their time on earth. Bill demonstrated the pliable nature of the synthetic flesh by pulling back a big flap of skin from his neck, revealing a white substance that resembled marshmallows. He then pressed the skin flap back into place, adjusting it with a slight motion of his fingers that erased any hint of seam where the flesh had been pried away. Seeing that apparently smooth, unblemished flesh had creeped Jack out a little.

Bills personality, on the other hand, put Jack completely at ease. He was so amiable, so easygoing and open about who and what he was. Jack found himself buying Bill's explanation of his presence—and, by extension, the presence of the other visitors—on Earth.

Earth, Bill said, was one of a handful of planets popular as a relocation choice for retirees from his world. Earth' atmosphere, he said, was more hospitable than that of his own world, which had become poisoned through too many centuries of industrial emissions so noxious and extreme they made the pollution problems here seem as harmless as a bath in a natural spring. We think of Earth, Bill told him, the way many humans think of Hawaii. A paradise.

So Jack let it go. He liked Bill. He believed his story.

It was really too bad he'd turned to be such a lying sack of alien shit.

He was also late.

Jack looked at the fake-gold-plated Rolex (Tijuana-issue) strapped around his left wrist and sighed. He was in a booth at the Gold Rush, a once-notorious Nashville dive that had recently undergone an extensive renovation in an effort to attract a more upscale clientele. Jack liked dives. He wasn't an upscale kind of guy. The Gold Rush had once been his favorite hometown watering hole. He did not care for the refurbished and sparkling clean new version. That it had kept the name of the old joint seemed a travesty.

However, it did possess a strategic value the Sherlock Holmes Pub lacked. His gaze went back to the plate-glass window that provided an excellent view of the sidewalk and the street beyond. There would be no sneak attack this time.

Jack reclined slightly in the booth and studied the passerby, searching for any hint of alien presence. He was pretty sure the people walking by were all human, or at least of earthly origin. The people out and about in this early dusk hour were mostly attractive young people, college students out to drink and hook up.

One slim young blonde in a tan miniskirt and white blouse stopped in midstride and turned to look through the window. Her gaze went right to Jack and she smiled. Jack returned the smile. She was a stunner. Her shiny hair was pulled back in a shorn ponytail, exposing delicate earlobes pierced by glittering diamond studs.

Jack's right hand curled about the handle of the .45 laying on the booth bench.

The blonde's smile tilted higher on the left side, becoming a smirk. She raised a hand and waggled a forefinger at him, and mouthed the words, "Naughty, naughty."

Jack swallowed hard and began to raise the .45.

The blonde leapt at the plate-glass window and crashed through it, landing cat-like on her feet as glass shards flew over the bar and skittered over the hardwood floor. Jack slid out of the booth and aimed the gun at the girl as startled patrons screamed, gibbered, and scrambled to get out of the line of fire.

The girl rose to a standing position, brushed glass out of her hair, and smiled again as she began to walk in an unhurried way toward Jack.

Jack thumbed back the .45's hammer and said, "Don't think I won't shoot a dame. I've done it before and I'll do it again. So stop right there, okay?"

The girl chuckled. "Dame? Honestly. Newsflash, big fella, it's a new century. You ought to upgrade your lingo."

She was still coming toward him, still in that deliberate way—not too fast, not too slow. In another moment or so she'd be right in front of him. The thought made Jack grit his teeth. A part of him really hated to ruin something so aesthetically pleasing, but a bigger part of him did not relish the idea of being torn apart by an alien. He squeezed the .45's trigger, sending a bullet straight toward the tip of that button-cute nose.

There was a flash of motion, then the girl was standing there with her hand cupped in front of her face.

Jack grimaced. "Aw, shit."

She opened her hand and the bullet tumbled harmlessly to the floor.

Her smirk deepened. "Want to try again?"

Jack lowered the gun. "How did you do that? The other ones couldn't"

"Mere foot soldiers. Hired hands. The interstellar equivalent of brainless, inbred rednecks. In retrospect, sending them against the likes of Jack Grimm and his compatriots wasn't the wisest course of action." She licked her lips and eyed him up and down. "I should've handled things personally from the beginning."

Jack frowned. "Who are you?"

The girl laughed. "You previously knew me as 'Bill.'"

Talk about your fucked-up paradigm shifts. Knowing the embodiment of hotness standing before him had looked like his uncle the last time he'd seen her

him, it, whatever...

abruptly rendered the frankly appraising way she…it…was sizing him up infinitely less sexy.

"Huh." He returned the useless .45 to his shoulder rig and straightened his jacket. "Well…um…Bill."

The girl/alien/whatsit tittered. "Call me Candi, with an i."

"I think not. You should go with Jill. Bill, Jill. Get it? There's a symmetry there, makes things less confusing for the rest of us." Jack chuckled. "Relatively speaking, we humans don't change genders with such ease."

She smiled. "More's the pity. Would make the dull little lives you dumb animals lead more interesting."

"Dumb animals, eh?" Jack smirked. "If we're so uninteresting, why the slave trade? Would seem to be a contradiction there, Jill."

The alien laughed softly. "Not at all. You're pathetic beings through and through, but useful in performing menial tasks, and amusing when made to perform in certain ways." She laughed again. "You make good pets."

Jack grimaced. “Don’t go quoting Porno For Pyros at me. That alone is grounds for termination with extreme prejudice.”

“Such a funny man, Mr. Grimm. But your jokes won’t save you.”

“There’s no need for threats, Jill. I think we can resolve this matter peacefully.”

The alien smiled. “You lie. And stop calling me that.”

Jack coughed. “Look, here’s the thing. Police will be here soon. Thanks to this…er…ruckus you’ve caused we can’t very well conduct negotiations at this location.”

“There will be no negotiations, human.”

She took a slow step toward him, then another, swinging her hips sinuously.

“Oh?” Jack took a shaky step backward, sweat starting to form on his upper lip.

“Mm-hmm.” She nodded and did that extraordinarily disconcerting lip-licking thing again, though now she looked more like a predator sizing up dinner than a seductress. “This time I’ll just rip off your head and be done with it.”

“What about the cops.”

She shrugged. “I’ll rip their heads off, too.”

“Great.” Jack grunted humorless laughter. “At least you’ve got it all thought out.”

She smiled. “Yes, I’m very thorough, Jack. Unlike you.” She laughed again as she neared him—she was almost close enough now to pounce on him. “You were so very easy to dupe before. You should’ve investigated further. Such a sloppy work ethic. And look at you now, caught so thoroughly unprepared and off-guard.” She sneered and shook her head, disdain evident in the curl of her lip. “You deserve to die this way.”

Jack smile. “Probably. But it’s not happening today.”

She threw her head back and laughed, a lilting sound full of girlish contempt. A perfect pose for the moment, really, Jack decided, as Andy swung the axe in a perfect arc and lopped the alien’s head off its shoulders. The head flew to the left and landed on a table amidst a platter of nachos and salsa dip. The head, still sentient, hissed and the headless body lurched at Jack with outstretched hands. Jack stumbled backward as Andy raised the axe high over his head and brought it down with great force, cleaving the head straight through the middle. The two halves toppled sideways, one into a plate of nachos, the other into the dip, white goo mingling with salsa in a way that made Jack's stomach churn.

The headless body sagged, then fell limp to the ground, the outstretched fingers of one immaculately manicured hand brushing the cuff of Jack's trousers. Jack kicked the hand away, heaved a relieved sigh, and looked at Andy. "You waited long enough to make your move brother."

Andy removed the ballcap he'd been wearing and sailed it over the bar. He then peeled away the fake dark beard and let it flutter to the ground. "That's where you're wrong, Jack. I had to play the part of the cowering bartender long enough to allow the creepy crawly to believe you were defenseless. Any sooner, and she would've still been on-guard for a rear flank attack.

Jack indicated the axe with a nod. "Good call on the axe."

Andy smiled. "Yeah, a much quicker and more efficient kill-method."

"At least in close quarters."

Jack's gaze went to the shattered window and the people milling about on the sidewalk. Two coppers stood among them, listening impatiently to the excited jabbering of witnesses. The boys in blue abruptly drew their weapons and moved toward the bar's entrance.

Andy followed Jack's gaze and said, "We really ought to get out of here. Can't afford to be dallying with the puppet authorities. Our work's not done yet."

By the time the police entered the Gold Rush, Jack and Andy were gone.

6.
Team Grimm Assembles

A homeless man awoke from a bad dream to face a waking nightmare. The largest and scariest-looking dog Duke Carlyle had ever seen growled at him, its black lips peeling back to reveal teeth that were abnormally long and sharp. Some wispy substance puffed out of its flaring nostrils.

Steam.

Not exhaled breath fogging in cold air, but honest-to-God actual STEAM.

Well, that just wasn't possible. No animal Duke knew of breathed anything other than oxygen. So Duke decided there was only one possible explanation for the impossible vision before him—the pooch from hell was a hallucination, just the latest in a long series of phantasmagorical delusions generated by his terminally booze-damaged alkie brain. It wasn't unusual for Duke to snap awake and see things that looked like demons or werewolves tearing apart helpless, screaming victims.

Things that clearly couldn't be real. Like this here hell-pooch.

So Duck did what he always did in these situations—he took a big slug of warm booze from his paper bag covered bottle of Nightrain and passed out again.

Lucien stopped growling the moment the old bum started snoring again. He considered barking to wake him again, or perhaps even taking a small bite of his flesh, but instantly dismissed these possibilities as untenable. Making a lot of scary hellhound noises hadn't worked the first time, and even the tiniest nip of the man's filth-covered flesh could trigger a hunger for more. That most primal part of his nature, the need to rip open living flesh and feel the warm blood of an innocent soul filling his mouth, was a wild thing that required a vigilant, intensely focused effort of will to control. 'Innocence' was a relative term, of course, perhaps even more so than usual in this case, but this walking human casualty was no adversary, no threat. Therefore he was off-limits, at least as long as the hellhound wished to remain on the side of the righteous—and he did, fervently so. Lucien didn't like to consider what might happen if his resolve ever faltered. Not that he needed to think about it. He knew what could happen.

I'd be Damned again.

My opportunity for Redemption gone forever...

So Lucien did the only thing he could do—he seized a mouthful of the old man's dirty clothes, and dragged him across the abandoned warehouse's pothole-dotted parking lot, depositing him behind an overturned trash can next to the rusted chain-link fence that ringed the gone-to-seed property. The man remained in a deep alcoholic slumber the whole way, even when his head thumped in and out of the occasional pothole

Lucien trotted back to the property's rear entrance, where he sat back on his hind legs and hoped no one inside had witnessed his work to clear the area outside the warehouse.

A nearby patch of air shimmered and grew black at the center.

Jack and Andy stepped out of the portal, both of them carrying pump-action shotguns. Jack had an extra weapon slung over his shoulder. Lucien shifted to his human form and took the second shotgun from Jack.

Lucien jacked a round into the chamber. "We ready to do this thing?"

Andy O'Day removed the cigarette dangling from the corner of his mouth and exhaled a thin stream of smoke. "Just about. We're not all here yet."

A moment after Andy's portal closed, the air where it'd opened grew hot again. Then a black slash in the fabric of reality opened, and Raven Rainbolt stepped through it. She made a hand gesture and the slash closed like a zipper. She was dressed all in black and was carrying an Ingram M10 submachine gun. A band of extra clips was slung over her shoulder and knotted at the waist.

Raven worked a different kind of magic than that practiced by Andy O'Day. She drew upon entirely different types of energies, and her method of traveling through the spaces between worlds was also vastly different. It was like literally moving through a dark hallway. That obliteration of consciousness that occurred with Andy's portals wasn't there. Jack frequently wished she'd teach the method to Andy, but didn't want to instigate a conflict of magical ideologies.

Lucien glanced at his shotgun, then nodded at Raven's weapon. "No fair. I want one of those."

Jack laughed. "Maybe next time, pal." He chambered a round too, then propped the gun's barrel over his shoulder and fished his cigarettes from a jacket pocket. Jack always had a smoke in the last moments before heading into a firefight; it helped calm his nerves. He fired a smoke up with his Zippo and looked beyond Lucien at the warehouse. "You sure this is the place, then?"

Lucien nodded. "Positive."

Jack took another drag off his cigarette, nodding as he exhaled more smoke. "The scent is that strong? You followed it here all the way from Bill's apartment?"

Lucien nodded again. "Their stench is almost overwhelming, at least when I'm in full-hound mode. Followed it like a beacon. They had some people keeping watch outside, armed guards." He grinned. "They're no longer a factor."

Jack let his half-smoke cigarette fall to the cracked and faded asphalt, extinguishing the still-glowing ember beneath the heel of a wingtip. "Let's do this." He looked at Raven. "It's your time to shine, Rave."

Raven remained expressionless as she strode past the men, climbed the short set of stairs to the back entrance, and positioned herself to aim a kick at the steel door.

Lucien frowned again. "Why is Raven taking the lead?"

Jack smirked. "You'll see."

Raven let out a grunt as her right foot shot forward with tremendous force and knocked the door off its hinges.

Lucien said, "Oh."

Jack chuckled. "Yeah, but there's another reason, too. Let's go."

Raven moved through the dark opening and into the warehouse. The men clambered up the steps and followed her into the darkness.

7.
Full-Tilt Rock and Roll

The threaded barrel of Raven's Ingram M10 was fitted with a Sionics suppressor. The weapon made a flat, snapping sound when she fired half a clip into the face of the first alien they encountered. The thing's head nearly disintegrated, spewing white goo as it toppled to the concrete floor.

Jack's voice was a barely audible whisper in the darkness: "*That's* why."

Raven remained on point as they moved deeper into the warehouse, moving in crouches as they progressed from one row of steel shelving to another. She dispatched five more alien guards with the same lethal efficiency. Each of the men fleetingly wondered whether the slightly built (but deceptively powerful) girl would accomplish this entire mission single-handedly.

For his part, Jack sincerely hoped not. He admired the hell out of Raven, but his male ego reacted in typical fashion, urging him to take out his share of bad guys before the evening's festivities were finished. He managed to suppress the urge, an all-too-rare case of common sense winning out over his baser impulses. Heavily armed though they were, this was an extraordinarily dangerous situation they'd walked into. Better by far to proceed with relative stealth, allowing Raven to pick off stray aliens with her Ingram, than letting loose with a barrage of attention-drawing shotgun blasts.

The darkness began to fade as they moved closer to the warehouse's center, where banks of flickering florescent lights gleamed overhead. They reached the last row of shelving and crouched down behind a rusting forklift.

Jack's blood boiled as they surveyed the scene at the heart of the warehouse. Pushed against the far wall were the remnants of some sort of assembly line. The warehouse's center floor area had been given over to an array of gleaming metal tables. Each had a naked, drooling human strapped to it. Aliens in white cloaks stood over the tables, poking and prodding at the bound humans with various instruments. The men and women on the table barely reacted, even when something sharp was inserted into their flesh.

Drugged, Jack thought, his teeth grinding.

More humans crouched in cages suspended by chains from the ceiling. Men and women, even a few children. All of them nude, all of them drugged to insensibility. Armed guards patrolled the perimeter of what Jack instantly thought of as the "operating theater." There were maybe a dozen of them in all, each of them carrying rifles or handguns. Jack began to smile as he studied them. They were sloppy. They didn't expect intruders, so they weren't looking for any. They milled about like bored high school students lounging outside the cafeteria between classes, talking and occasionally laughing.

Jack looked at Andy and held out a hand. "Stunners."

Any nodded and reached inside his jacket. He snapped a stun grenade off a strap and pressed it into Jack's open palm. He passed another to Lucien, and another to Raven, then palmed one for himself.

Jack said, "These bastards aren't half as disciplined as the worst of Saddam's front-line conscripts. Look, the one group of complacent sons of bitches is wandering back to the other group of complacent sons of bitches." He looked at Andy again. "How's your pitching arm?"

Andy flexed his shoulder, limbering up. "Pretty good, I think."

Raven nodded.

Lucien grunted an affirmation.

Jack pulled the pin on his grenade and the others did the same.

"Count of three."

Jack counted off, then leapt to his feet, his arm coming forward in the same motion, sending a fist-sized black blob hurtling through the air. Three more followed it in similar arcs. The alien guards didn't realize anything was amiss until the grenades clattered on the floor and rolled between their legs—and by then it was too late. The M429s erupted in nearly simultaneous blasts of flame and smoke. The guards pitched to the ground, most of them losing their weapons in the process. Jack and his gang of liberators charged out of their hiding place, speeding past the startled "doctors" and moaning "patients" en route to the still-stunned guards.

A couple of them had already managed to stagger to their feet and begin to raise their weapons. Jack aimed his shotgun and squeezed the trigger, blowing apart the first one's head. The roar of another shotgun, this one wielded by Lucien, blew apart the neck of the second. It remained upright and continued its labored effort to bring its weapon to bear, but Lucien just chambered another round and shot it point-black in the face. Most of the remaining guards stayed on the ground, still stunned, a few even holding their trembling hands up in supplication. Andy leveled the barrel of his weapon at the back of one's head, then squeezed the trigger. It jerked once and slumped to the ground. His face expressionless, he moved to the alien next to it and killed it, too. Jack and Lucien followed his lead, systematically executing the remaining guards. They'd discussed it beforehand—none of them were to be left alive.

Raven left them to it and hurried after the fleeing faux-doctors. She was faster than a normal human, but that was because she *wasn't* a normal human. The descendent (from her father's side) of a refugee clan of wizards from another galaxy, she had alien blood flowing through her veins, too. Which kind of made things more personal for her—these interplanetary thugs offended both aspects of her nature.

She swung the Ingram back and forth in wide arcs, taking most of them down within moments. She ejected the spent clip, snapped another one in pace as she pounded after the few still-mobile aliens, and started firing again. The final three aliens fell to the floor and Raven quickly finished them off, obliterating most of their heads with close-range bursts from the Ingram. She then went back to the initial group of wounded white-cloaked aliens and used another full clip to do them in. When it was done, she flicked the gun's safety on and returned to where the men were standing.

Jack looked at her. "You okay?"

A corner of Raven's mouth twitched. "All in a day's work, boss."

Lucien's gaze swept over the rows of gleaming tables and strapped-down slaves. He glanced at the ceiling, too. "Okay, so the bad guys are vanquished. That was the easy part. What do we do about these poor bastards?"

Andy flipped open a cell phone. "Got it covered, mate."

Jack grinned. "Come on, Lucien. You knew he'd say that."

Lucien shook his head. "The mysterious, all-knowing

Svengali thing freaks me out a little sometimes."

Jack said, "Yeah?"

Andy moved away from his friends, turning his back to them and talking in hushed tones for a minute or two. Then he turned back to them and snapped the cell phone shut. "A clean-up crew and medics are on the way." His gaze flicked upward. "Let's do our part and figure out how to get those people down from there."

Before Jack could ask how they were supposed to do that, a portal opened and a big man in a blue-and-white Hawaiian shirt stepped through it. He was followed by a team of white-suited men and women carrying first aid kits and other medical supplies.

Jack blinked rapidly for a few moments. "Well…that was fast."

The white suits immediately started attending to the people on the tables, and Mr. Hawaiian Shirt came over and bear-hugged Andy O'Day. Andy slapped the other man's back. "Good to see you again, mate."

They separated and Andy said, "Jack, I'd like you to meet a friend of mine. This is Fred Grimm." Andy winked. "No relation. I think."

"Huh." Jack shook the affable man's hand. "Are you sure we're not related?"

Fred's eyes twinkled with amusement. "Oh, pretty sure.' He half-turned away from them, taking in the totality of the situation. His voice took on a graver tone. "We'll handle all this. Go on and get out of here."

Andy glanced again at the caged humans hanging from the ceiling. "But—"

"You've done enough tonight. We've got this covered." Fred grinned again. "Even superheroes need a little rest."

Jack frowned. "Superheroes? Hey, listen—"

Andy clapped a hand on his shoulder. "Don't argue with him, brother. My advice, someone calls you a superhero, go with it. There are worse things to be."

Jack let out a sigh. The man had a point.

Better heroic than Damned anyway.

"Okay. Fine. Let's get out of here." He looked at Fred, studying him intently for a moment. "We'll talk again, you and I."

Fred smiled. "Oh, I don't doubt that."

The members of the Grimm Detective Agency walked out of the warehouse exiting through the rear door Raven had kicked down less than half an hour earlier. They moved slowly down the steps, each of them feeling that deep tiredness that comes in the wake of surviving a battle, a sapping of energy that had more to do with the relief of high-level stress than with physical exertion.

As they reached the parking lot, a hunched figure lurched toward them out of the darkness and Jack instinctively raised the shotgun.

But Lucien pushed the barrel down. "Don't."

The figure came closer and Jack saw it was just a grime-covered man in filthy clothes. The man staggered like a drunk, and in a moment Jack realized it was because he was in fact, very, very drunk. Jack shuddered, and a vague chill settled in his gut. A part of him sometimes suspected he'd wind up like this poor fellow one day.

Duke Carlyle gasped at the sight of all the weaponry. "Don't shoot me."

Jack said, "Go sleep it off elsewhere, fella."

Duke squinted at him. "Who're you to tell me what to do?" His gaze went to each of them in turn, lingering for a moment on Lucien. He frowned. "Why ain't you got no clothes on, boy?"

Lucien smiled.

And shifted to hound mode.

Duke fainted.

Lucien reverted to human form. "That's why."

Jack sighed. "What do we do with this guy? Leave him here? It's not like he's got a home to go to."

Andy shook his head. "You have something of a point, but that's not what superheroes do."

Jack rolled his eyes. "Again with that nonsense."

Andy said, "We'll get him to a shelter, see he's looked after, at least for tonight."

Jack was silent for a long moment. He looked up at the sky and tried to see any stars through the haze of city lights and pollution. He didn't see any. Not a single one. He could almost believe this world he inhabited was the only world, that the billions of living things inhabiting this sphere were the only living things in all existence.

But, of course, he knew that wasn't true.

He looked at the unconscious drunk again and said, "Okay."

Because tonight he knew only one true thing for absolutely certain.

Tonight they were heroes.

8.
Unfinished Business

Lucy Martin grinned and plunged her fangs into the girl's tender, exposed neck. The euphoria hit her immediately, faster and more powerful than the strongest drug rush, and she slurped the girl's blood greedily, drinking and drinking, until she'd drained her. She relinquished the girl's limp form reluctantly, allowing it to fall to the bloodied sofa.

Lucy stood up and released an exultant hiss of satisfaction.

She heard a sudden sound, the creak of a floorboard, and whirled to face the interloper.

Jack Grimm sighed. "You killed her."

Lucy grinned. "Yes. And now I'll kill you."

Jack moved further into the room, his deliberate movements indicating wariness of the vampire's power but no fear. "Tell me something, Lucy. How does it feel to become what you hated. Do you think it's right? Is there even one shred of humanity left in you, one tiny piece of your soul that doesn't want this, that wants you to stop?"

Lucy grinned again. She licked blood from her lips. "No. The weak, helpless little girl who came begging for your help is no more. I'm better now." She took a step toward Jack. "You shouldn't judge me. You have no clue how good it feels to drink and kill. Maybe I'll show you. Maybe I'll turn you, make you my slave. Did you know vampires can enslave those they turn?"

She kept coming at him, her dark, soulless eyes gleaming.
Jack said, "Yeah, I know that."

Lucy laughed. "And maybe that's why you came back. Maybe you want to live forever like me. Or maybe you just want *me*." She giggled. "Oh, don't think I didn't see the dirty old man lust in your eyes every time you looked at me. Give in to it, Jack. Let me take you, let me make your darkest, fondest dreams come true."

Jack shook his head. "You're wrong, Lucy."

The vampire smirked. "Oh."

"Yeah." Jack brought the crossbow from behind his back, aimed it with as much precision as he'd ever aimed his .45, and said, "You're not gonna live forever."

He clicked the trigger and the wooden bolt shot forward, piercing Lucy's heart.

She glanced at the protruding bolt, then looked at Jack with an expression of wide-eyed, beseeching terror. "No."

Jack sighed and lowered the crossbow.

Lucy's eyes went blank and she fell dead to the floor.

Jack regarded her a moment longer, then walked out of the house. He stood in the backyard and smoked a cigarette, silently contemplating the starry night sky.

9.
Angst

The next afternoon Jack and Andy were sitting at the bar in the Sherlock Holmes Pub. Andy was drinking Irish whiskey and Jack was nursing his second pint of the day. They'd already laid down their usual big tips, their way of thanking the bar's staff for their usual lack of cooperation with the authorities after the big shootout in the street the week before.

Andy said, "You did what you had to do."

Jack sipped his stout. It tasted bitter. "You're always saying that."

Andy chuckled. "And I'm always right."

Jack nodded. "Maybe." He looked at his brother. His friend. "They're still after me, you know. Satan's people."

Andy stared into his dwindling glass of whiskey. "They'll always be after you, Jack. Until your dying breath. But you already knew that."

Jack sighed. "Yeah. But sometimes I think how nice it'd be to…" He signed again. "I don't know, live a normal life. To not feel constantly hounded and hunted. To not feel the weight of worlds on my shoulders."

Andy finished his drink and pushed the empty glass forward for a refill.

He looked at Jack, smiling but with a hint of sadness in his eyes. "It's okay to dream, brother, but you and I both know you were born for this. So was I."

Jack chuckled bitterly. "Slaves of destiny?"

Andy received his refilled glass with a smile and a nod, then raised it for a toast. "To the very end."

They clinked glasses.

Someone sounded a few tinkling notes on the piano. Jack and Andy swiveled on their chairs and grinned at the sight of Raven sitting on the piano bench. She played a few more notes, her confidence growing, then began to sing the opening lines of "Always Look On The Bright Side Of Life."

Before long, everyone in the Sherlock Holmes Pub had joined in.

Jack's voice was the loudest of them all.

HELL AIN'T A BAD PLACE TO BE

The last day of John Marlowe's mortal life began with a hangover. He woke up, opened his bleary eyes, took a good look around, shuddered at the disarray in the bedroom, and went back to sleep for a few more hours. When he got up again, he shrugged into the clothes he'd worn the day before, stumbled into the kitchen, and opened the fridge.

It was still there.

The severed head sat in an aluminum pie tray, the ragged stump of its neck buried in a layer of cookie dough. Strands of blood-flecked blond hair dangled through the shelf slats, brushing the plastic lid of a bowl of tuna salad.

"Fuck. I really did it."

John Marlowe was forty-two. He hadn't killed anyone since his early twenties. In those days, he'd had some level of ambition, as well as a young man's elevated sense of his own importance in the grand scheme of things. He'd wanted to make his mark in the world. Do something big and become famous. As a teenager he learned to play guitar and tried starting a band. The rock star life seemed like a good gig. Groupies and all the drugs you could handle. Problems set in when he discovered he couldn't sing or write even one half-decent song. So he gave that up and decided to become a novelist. A celebrated man of letters. He imagined a different kind of fame and fortune. National Book Awards and interviews on NPR. The bigger literary names even had their own kind of groupies. Brainy women who would pin their hair back and wear owl's-eye glasses, hide their sleek and wanton bodies in modest clothes. The sexy librarian type. But in the bedroom they'd be foul-mouthed, dominating hellcats. If anything, it was an even more appealing prospect than the abandoned dream of busty, miniskirt-wearing rock star groupies, all of whom would have been empty-headed bottle-blond bimbos straight out of a 1980's Poison video. Not that there was anything wrong with empty-headed bottle-blond bimbos. It was just a question of whether you more enjoyed the refined taste of an expensive wine or the simpler taste of a cheap domestic beer. There was a time and place for both, and at that point in his young existence John had decided he was going to be the kind of man who preferred the finer things in life. All he had to do to make this happen was sit down and write the Great American Novel, and perhaps follow it up with maybe half a dozen lesser novels over the course of the next thirty years or so to keep the cash and lit-slut groupies rolling in.

He sat down to write the novel.

Wrote one page.

Read it through a dozen times or so.

And decided it was again time to reevaluate his goals in life.

Still thinking in terms of groupies and fame and fortune, he toyed with the idea of becoming an actor. He went so far as to take a few acting classes. Three classes, to be exact, each of them a study in awkwardness and boredom.

By then he was close to accepting he had no ability whatever in any of the creative fields. He could maybe go into politics. He was young and good-looking, and possessed more than enough personal charisma to get by. He could be a congressman. A senator. Hell, he could be president. The job clearly didn't require brains. If anything, he was overqualified.

But politics bored him even more than acting, so fuck that.

The reality that banging bimbos could be something of a potential liability in the political arena was somewhat of a deciding factor, as well.

And then it happened, the moment that changed his life.

The goddamn epiphany.

He could be a serial killer.

And not just any ordinary dumb bastard of a serial killer. The usual guys in that field were greasy dullards. Ugly bastards who wore over-sized glasses with thick lenses. Sexual predators driven by anger and frustration, who killed because no woman in her right mind would ever voluntarily give up the goods to a guy like that. Those guys, they didn't exactly stir the imagination. Sure, every once in a while someone more interesting came along, someone like Ted Bundy. Now there was a guy who was legitimately a legend in the annals of serial killing. Some guys had killed more women than Ted, but few had ever done it with the pizazz of the Deliberate Stranger. But even he had botched it all in the end. John decided he would follow in Bundy's footsteps only to a degree. He would do everything his new hero had done right, avoid his missteps, and elevate the killing game to a whole new level. And by the time he was done, he meant to be the world's most prolific and creative serial killer ever. Books would be written about him. Movies made. He would finally be a celebrity of a sort. And, hell, some of the more interesting and charismatic serial killers, Ted included, even had their own groupies.

Yep, on paper it all looked very positive.

That summer, at the age of twenty-two, he killed three women. He did his homework so well beforehand that he was never a suspect in any of the ensuing investigations. He was never questioned. None of the suspect sketches the police circulated ever looked remotely like him. And yet, the killings had been public and spectacularly gruesome. The corpses were decapitated and mutilated in myriad creative ways. None of this strangling the lass and ditching her body in a remote patch of wilderness never to be discovered jazz. This was to be a very open campaign of shock and awe horror. And it worked. The local media went apoplectic after the first killing. The national press got in on the act after the third victim was discovered. He was dubbed The Little Rock Madman, not a bad serial killer name. All was going very much according to plan.

Except for one little thing.

John just wasn't enjoying the work very much.

Oh, he'd gotten a real high from successfully pulling off

the first job. In those first moments of his new existence as a murderer, he'd been certain he'd found at last his true calling in life. But the high faded faster than he expected and his sleep that night was disrupted by nightmares. He chalked it up to first time pangs of conscience. Not even that, really. This was just social conditioning, a mental and chemical reflex, something that would surely fade as the work became more routine. So he pressed ahead with his plan. But the nightmares and sleep disruptions got exponentially worse after he offed the second and third girls. After the third one, he got blind drunk and woke up in a pool of his own piss and vomit in an alley behind a Little Rock dive bar. He woke up screaming and crying every night for months. Turned out he had a real conscience after all. The faces of the dead women haunted him day and night. His day job suffered. He dropped out of grad school. And his life continued on a grim downward spiral until the night he got down on his knees in yet another backstreet alley and begged God and his victims for forgiveness.

His life changed after that night. He did everything he could think of to atone, short of turning himself in and signing a confession. He went back to school and graduated with honors. He became a very successful man. A wealthy man. He donated tons of money to victims groups and death penalty advocates. He went to church twice a week and continued to pray every day for forgiveness. Years went by. Decades. Enough time that the killings he'd done that long ago summer began to seem like something he must have imagined, something that couldn't possibly be real. Except that every once in a while, even all these years later, the local media would dredge the whole thing up again, reminding the public that the Little Rock Madman had never been caught. Even so, the passage of time and his acts of contrition combined to convince him that he had truly transformed himself. He wasn't really a monster. That bloody summer had ultimately been nothing more than a blip in an otherwise exemplary life, a wrong path he'd been wise enough to quickly abandon.

An impression that had lasted until roughly one week prior to today.

John stared at his wife's severed head and said, "You fucking bitch."

He'd come home early from work that day and caught her in bed with a much younger man. A large black man with a bodybuilder's physique and a model's chiseled face. Later he learned the man was an expensive male prostitute. Which explained Linda's reaction upon seeing him in the bedroom doorway. There had been no shame. No quick, startled disengagement of the two sleek, sweaty bodies. Instead she'd yelled at him to get out of the room so she could finish. Turned out she'd just wanted to get her money's worth. John had retreated to his study down the hall, where he cracked the seal on a bottle of very fine old scotch and settled into his leather executive's chair to listen to his wife's orgasmic screams. The screams interested him. They were high and shrill, not entirely dissimilar to the screams made by the victims of the Little Rock Madman. The thought made him frown. Linda never sounded like that when he was putting it to her.

He started thinking about killing her after that first sip of scotch. The thought seemed to come from nowhere and sent a shudder of revulsion rippling through his whole body. He'd had no conscious, active thoughts about killing anyone in twenty years. The scotch turned sour in his stomach and he felt bile at the back of his throat.

At some point the screams from the bedroom faded and stopped. A little later he heard muted conversation in the hallway. Then male laughter and feminine giggling. They were laughing at him. The insight did nothing to lighten his thoughts. Then she came into the study, a robe cinched tight around her shapely body, and made several declarations. They were not going to get divorced. Of course not. She enjoyed her position in the community too much. He was never going to breathe a word of this to anyone. She would continue to screw the thousand-dollar-a-pop prostitute twice a week, and she would continue to sample any other strange flesh that caught her fancy, including John's young lesbian niece, who she'd apparently been corrupting for months. And furthermore, he was never going to have sex with her again, because he was just no good at it. Not only that, but he was not allowed to have affairs of his own. She would not have anyone in town talking about her behind her back. Then she pried the bottle of scotch from his shaking fingers and told him he was not allowed to drink anymore. Still more ultimatums followed, each more galling than the last.

He was initially defiant. "You realize this is ludicrous, right? What makes you think I'll be a good little doggie and do everything you say?"

She smirked and looked down her regal nose at him. "Because you talk in your sleep. Mr. Madman. Why, you're practically verbose."

John just stared at her, suddenly cold and dead inside.

"There are things you don't want people to know."

He stayed silent, struggled to breathe.

"Nasty things."

His fingers dug into his knees, made the bones grind.

"So, yes, I do think I have the leverage I need here." Her smirk deepened, became a look of utter, smug certainty. "I own you now, John. You're my little wind-up toy. Finish up whatever you're doing in here and come out to the kitchen. I'm going to write up a list of new chores for you."

She turned her back on him and sashayed back through the door, making a show of how little she feared the infamous Little Rock Madman.

John slumped in his chair.

His thoughts turned to murder again.

But that sense of revulsion was still there. He'd worked so hard to redeem himself. He just couldn't let himself succumb to the old demons. Not even at the cost of his own manhood and dignity. The dark thoughts nonetheless stayed with him in the days that followed, though he struggled hard against them, even in the face of so much deep humiliation. And it got worse. She kept doing things to deepen his shame. The worst was yesterday, when she made him watch her fuck the prostitute. They tied him to a chair in the bedroom, and then they did it all. Missionary position. Girl on top. From behind, with both anal and vaginal penetration. Reverse cowgirl and face-sitting. Jesus, but it just went on and fucking on. By the time the prostitute left, John had been reduced to a trembling lump of insensible flesh. Linda didn't free him from the chair until hours later. She then slapped him out of his stupor and ordered him to take out the trash and wash the dishes.

John did take out the trash.

Then he got into his Mercedes and drove far, far away from there. He stayed out for hours, drinking himself senseless in a succession of low-rent dives in the worst part of town. He didn't remember coming home. Didn't remember going to bed. But his sleep was tortured with nightmare visions of bloody murder. The images were so vivid and real. His wife dying horribly at his hands, tortured first, then chopped and diced into little pieces.

Turned out there was a reason the images were so damn vivid.

They were fucking real, man. Not nightmares at all, but memories.

John threw the refrigerator door shut.

He thought, *Well, that's it.*

There was no denying the truth of it. There was no coming back from this. It was the thing he'd told himself he couldn't live with if it happened again, and John had always been a man true to his word. He would honor this vow.

But first he would bear witness to the rest of his shame.

He shuffled out of the kitchen and made his way to the dining room. Here was where most of the action had occurred. John's knees went weak at the sight of the carnage. There were pieces of Linda on the dinner table. Her breasts on a ceramic plate. One looked to have been partially devoured. He saw fingers protruding from candle holders, each fingernail adorned with the shade of deep scarlet polish Linda favored. The lower half of her body was arranged with its legs spread in the center of the table. He supposed he'd climbed onto the table and defiled it at least once during the evening. What remained of her torso sat in a chair, a large knife protruding from the space between her missing breasts. And of course there was a simply amazing amount of blood splashed all over the room.

Feeling numb, John drank it all in.

It was incredible.

The Little Rock Madman had clearly not lost his gift for creative slaughter during his long period of inactivity. He even felt a strange sort of pride beneath the overwhelming sense of horror and failure.

The numbness faded.

A wash of nausea swept through him and he vomited profusely, the force of it sending him to his hands and knees. He heaved and heaved, spewing bile all over a severed big toe that had found its way to the floor. The spasms continued long after his stomach had emptied its contents. His joints and muscles ached with the pain of it, pain so overwhelming he actually welcomed it, because for a time it blocked out the reality of what he had done. But eventually the sickness gripping him faded and he was again forced to face the awful truth.

He got to his feet and staggered out of the room. His body reeled as he made his way through the big house, pitching side to side, hands held out to his sides in order to bounce off the walls and remain upright. Stumbling through the door to his study, he spied his leather chair and fell toward it with his arms extended, seeking it with the desperation of a shipwreck survivor grasping for the only life-preserver in sight. He made it to the chair, sat there slumped and panting for several minutes.

Many minutes passed. He began to regain some measure of physical and mental control. Then he set about doing the things he needed to do. He found a pad of paper and a pen, and he began to write the untold story of The Little Rock Madman. The rambling confession had more than enough details about the murders to convince authorities the real killer had at last been unmasked, albeit posthumously. The letter also contained heartfelt apologies to the families of his victims, and proclaimed that he would not ask for their forgiveness because he did not deserve it. Any of them were welcome to come to his grave to piss on it. He concluded by stating that while his wife had undeniably been a heartless bitch of truly epic proportions, she had not deserved to die. He apologized to her family and said that they, too, were welcome to piss on his grave.

He read the confession through two times, then signed it.

He reached for the bottle of old scotch Linda had pried from his fingers a week ago, but didn't pick it up, deciding he didn't deserve even this one last fleeting pleasure. Instead he opened the bottom drawer of his desk, removed the .44 Magnum from the lock box at the back, put the gun's barrel in his mouth, and squeezed the trigger. He didn't hear the gun's report or even really feel what the large-caliber bullet did to his head. The awesome destructive power of the weapon did its work too fast and too efficiently for that, triggering a brief geyser of blood and brains that splattered shelves of leather-bound books behind his desk.

The next thing he was aware of was music.

Crunchy, distorted guitar chords and a thumping drum beat.

In a moment he recognized the song as "Highway To Hell" by AC/DC. He had loved them as a teenager, but hearing this particular song now was not exactly the most reassuring thing he had ever experienced.

John opened his eyes and realized at once that he was in Hell.

At first blush it looked like any large metropolitan city. Buildings, the rumble of traffic, honking horns, and the buzz of nearby voices. He was standing on a sidewalk. A standard issue city sidewalk. This could have been a street in Manhattan. Maybe Greenwich Village. But then there were the obvious big differences. The street vendor selling fried human eyeballs from a cart across the street. The sign on a utility pole which read CITY MUTILATION ZONE. And the many creatures that could only be demons of various sorts in the mix of milling pedestrians. He looked up and saw the roiling red sky and the sickle-shaped black moon that hung there.

He pinched himself and said, "Ouch."

He patted his face and the top of his head, which was somehow intact, and that was quite a remarkable thing indeed, given that he'd just fired a bullet through it. But there was no denying the physical reality. He was alive again. In Hell, but alive.

He shook his head. "I'll be damned."

A hooker in miniskirt, high heels, and red fishnets paused in the process of strutting past him, turning a face toward him that looked like it had been boiled in acid. "We're all Damned. You want a blowjob?"

John decided her face probably had actually been boiled in acid. "Um...no. Thanks anyway."

The hooker's face twisted, forming an expression that might have been a sneer. It was hard to tell through all the scarring. "You sure? You don't know what you're missing. Ask anybody, they'll tell you. I give the best head of any whore in Hell."

Against his will, an image of his erect cock wedged in the scary black slit that was the hooker's mouth formed in John's head. He grimaced. "No, sorry. I, uh, no offense or anything, but..."

The hooker reached into the little handbag slung over her shoulder and removed something. He heard a click of a button and saw a shiny blade pop open. The hooker brandished the switchblade and said, "We're going into that alley behind you. I'm gonna blow you and then I'm gonna cut your dick off for a trophy." Her face twisted again, the scarred flesh arranging itself into something that could theoretically have been a smile. "And there ain't shit you can do about it."

John swallowed hard. "Um..."

Run, he thought. *Just run.*

Another second and he might have bolted, but the soft, sultry voice to his right stopped him. "Get lost, whore. This one's mine."

Great.

The whores of Hell were arguing over him, and he hadn't been here five minutes yet. Not an auspicious start. He was feeling a bit like a piece of meat. It was not a feeling he enjoyed. "Look—"

He turned to address the second whore, but the words died in his throat with a gurgle. He went cold inside and again felt the urge to bolt. The second woman was not another cheap streetwalker. She was gorgeous, with long, lustrous blond hair and an exquisite face worthy of the cover of Vogue. The body was just as stunning, sleek and slender but with lush curves and ample breasts. It was the kind of body meant for modeling swimsuits. The dress she wore looked stylish and sexy, not at all like anything a whore would have in her wardrobe. It looked expensive, as if it must have been purchased from one of Hell's most upscale boutiques. He knew nothing of the current fashion trends in Hell, but instinct told him this woman would always stand at its cutting edge. The backless black dress looked molded to her figure, a supple second skin that would be a pleasure and privilege to peel away from her creamy, unblemished flesh.

John felt the same instant, reflexive lust he'd felt the first time he'd seen her.

Which had been at a nightclub in Little Rock twenty years ago, the night before he hacked her into seemingly a million little pieces in that public park.

Her smile broadened, became truly radiant. "Hello, John. I knew you were coming. I can't tell you how good it is to see you again."

Beyond any shadow of a doubt, it was her.

Angela Willis.

A memory came to him. Angela's mother on the news, crying for the cameras, begging the police to do anything to catch the monster who had taken her baby.

John turned and ran.

He shoved his way through the crowd on the sidewalk with heedless abandon, knocking a fat man into a demon's back in the process. The demon turned, snarling as its black wings unfurled. Its mouth widened, the flesh displaying a shocking level of elasticity as the black maw grew to a size large enough to swallow the fat man's head, which it promptly did. John kept moving, turning his back on the demon as its flashing, razor-sharp teeth clamped together.

He glanced back twice to see if Angela was pursuing him, but he seemed to have lost her in the foot traffic. He slowed his pace and eventually came to a panting stop outside the open door of a rock club. Live music blared through the open door, filling this section of the street with its concussive beat. It was yet another AC/DC song. "Night Prowler." John frowned. It was obvious he was hearing live music and not a recording. But that voice...

Nah, couldn't be...

Curiosity and the need to find a place to hide and collect his wits drew him into the club. The place wasn't very big, a dark and grimy dive. There was a bar and a stage. Between them was a scattering of tables. The people sitting at the tables were drinking and watching the band, who were not AC/DC. The singer, though, was Bon Scott. No mistaking that guy for anyone else, and no mistaking that whiskey-drenched Scottish yowl. Some of the musicians in his backing band looked kind of familiar, too. A younger John Marlowe would likely have recognized them all on the spot.

"Night Prowler" ended and Scott interacted with the crowd, cracking jokes and engaging in witty and ribald banter with a large-breasted female in a miniskirt. The female was humanoid, but not human, with red eyes and tusks protruding from the corners of her mouth. Two small black wings, unnoticeable at first, were folded tight against the broad expanse of her back. John cringed at an impossible-sounding proposition made by the she-thing, then wandered over to the bar, slid onto a stool, and ordered a beer.

The bald and burly bartender crossed his massive tattooed forearms and sneered. "Ain't got no Guinness."

"Newcastle?"

"Nope."

"Spaten?"

"You ain't in Germany, dickhole."

"Harpoon IPA?"

"You really aren't getting the picture, are you?"

John rattled off a long list of other favorite brews, none of which were stocked at the Dirty Halo, which was the name of the place. "Look, can I just get a menu?"

The bartender picked up a glass and placed it under a tap. "Shut up, asshole." He flipped the taphead down and filled the glass with a rich, dark brew. He set the glass in front of John. "Drink that. You'll like it."

John picked up the glass, sniffed at it, and took a tentative sip. The sensation of the liquid on his tongue was exquisite. He showed the bartender an astonished expression. "Dear God, that is the best fucking beer I have ever fucking had."

The bartender smirked. "That's Gein's Mean Imperial Stout. Most popular beer in the Bathory district." The big man's brow creased. "You're new to the Mephistopolis, aren't you?"

John sampled some more beer and shivered at the heady taste. "Yeah. How did you know?"

The man laughed. "The freshly Damned are always fuckin' clueless, man."

John wasn't offended by the remark. "Makes sense. Listen, I just got here. Any idea where I should go from here? I mean..." He waved a hand at the club's open entrance, a vague gesture meant to encompass the whole of Hell itself. "...this is all sort of overwhelming. Hell is just this giant fucking city. There's all kinds of insane shit out there, but people have jobs. They go to clubs to see bands. So how do I fit in? Where will I live? Do I go to some kind of infernal temp agency?"

"This has all been arranged for you, John."

John jumped at the sound of her voice. The pint glass popped out of his grip and tumbled over, spilling stout all over the bar.

The bartender didn't look happy. In fact, he looked furious. But then his face turned pale. He unclenched his fists and bowed his head, mumbling words of terrified contrition, alternately referring to Angela as "My Lady" and "Your Highness."

John puzzled over the bartender's obsequious reaction, then looked at Angela. "I'm just not going to get away from you, am I?"

She sat on the stool next to him and placed a hand in his lap. "No, you won't." She laughed, and the sound was as he remembered it from that long ago night in the park before he revealed his true intentions. Soft and musical, like a feather tickling the pleasure centers of his brain. She massaged his crotch, stirring him to full arousal with an ease that belied the circumstances. "And believe me, John, you won't want to. I'm the personal concubine of a Grand Duke. I have an exalted position in this part of the Mephistopolis, with privileges that aren't available to most humans. I always get what I want, John. And what I want now is you."

He frowned. “I chopped your head off and had sex with your dead body. If what you say is true, you’re probably taking me back to your unholy castle or whatever to torture me for the rest of eternity. Right?”

She smiled as she tugged at his zipper tab. “Has it not occurred to you to wonder why I’m in Hell, John? After all, I was just an innocent victim of a horrible crime, right?”

John’s frown deepened. “Huh. Well, now that you mention it...”

“My name joined the endless list of the Eternally Damned the day I smothered my sick and elderly grandmother with a pillow. I was eight, John.” Her hand was inside his pants now. He gasped at the feel of her fingers curling around his stiff member. “The ‘accidental drowning’ of my little brother on our beach vacation a few years later was just icing on the Damnation cake. And for weeks I’d been imagining how I might get away with killing a pregnant co-worker when you came along and did what you did.” There was a strangely wistful note in her tone now. “Which was the best thing that ever happened to me.”

John gasped and gripped the edge of the bar as she continued to stroke him.

He looked at her and managed to speak between gasps. “Are you...fucking...kidding...me?

Another of those incredible laughs. “Oh, darling, I would never kid you. Life on the other side bored me so. All those repressed notions of right and wrong. It was stultifying. When you sent me here, you set me free.”

John whimpered. “I sent you to...Hell.”

She smiled and licked her lips. “Yes, and here I’ve flourished. Suddenly I found myself in a place where I was free to indulge all my darkest passions. Absolutely free to commit acts of atrocity I would never have dared imagining before. And I reveled in it, darling. I crushed the skulls of little children with bricks. Broiled a baby in an oven and fed it to its mother. Sawed off a man’s penis, cooked it, and fed it to him.”

John gasped again and slapped the top of the bar. “Holy shit, you are one sick bitch.”

She giggled, the little girlish quality of which was quite

disturbing juxtaposed against the recitation of purest evil spilling from her lovely mouth. "Yes, I am. I quickly became a rather notorious character, John, and soon caught the attention of District Commissioner of Torture Kennedy. From there I slept and murdered my way up the power hierarchy, eventually arriving at my current position as personal concubine to Grand Duke Dracul. I have riches beyond imagining at my disposal. I have a lover willing and able to give me everything I could ever want. Including you, John."

A corner of John's mouth quirked. "Me?"

She stopped stroking him and wrapped her fingers tighter around his cock, making him whimper again and slide toward the edge of the stool. "Yes. The Grand Duke's sources were able to pinpoint the precise moment and location of your arrival in Hell, and as a gift to me a document was filed with Luciferic bureaucracy allowing me to claim you as my own personal property."

She squeezed him harder and John's fingernails dug into the bar. "You mean...like...your slave?"

"Technically, yes."

John thought of his last week of mortal life and marriage with Linda.

So this was going to be his existence in Hell—an eternity of the same torment.

Well, he couldn't say he didn't deserve it, at least.

She giggled again. "Oh, relax. You're going to love it, seeing as I'll be fucking you half-blind a lot of the time. Do you know, John, that when you held me down in that park and showed me the meat cleaver, I knew I'd at last found a kindred soul? Oh, I was scared half to fucking death, but in that moment I knew you were like me inside. I wanted to tell you, but..." She shrugged, and there was something almost sad in her smile now. "Anyway, I don't think you would have listened. You were too focused on your work."

She relinquished her grip on his cock and John came explosively all over the front of the bar. He collapsed against the top of the bar and lay there in a shuddering, whimpering heap for several moments while Angela stroked his hair. The band launched into another song while she leaned close and cooed reassurances in his ear. When it was over, Angela took John by the hand and pulled him off the bar stool.

He still felt woozy and staggered along beside her as they left the Dirty Halo. "Where are we going?"

She smiled again as they came to a stop out on the sidewalk. "Home, John. I'm taking you to your new home. And there'll be a special surprise for you once we get there."

Surprise?

She saw his concerned expression and gave his arm a gentle squeeze. "You will love it. I promise."

"Okay. Whatever."

He looked up and saw huge winged creatures moving across the scarlet sky. His took another good look around. He saw thick clusters of black and impossibly tall skyscrapers in the distance. They dominated the skyline. He also saw the thick smokestacks of factories belching great billowing clouds of black, diseased smoke at the sky. The stench of decay permeated everything.

John looked at Angela. "What does 'City Mutilation Zone' mean?"

She laughed. "An institutionalized method of random slaughter. Nothing for you to worry about." She winked. "When you're with me, that is."

"I offed myself with a .44 caliber bullet. Probably took off the top of my head. So where's the giant fucking hole in my skull?"

"That was your mortal flesh, John. You have a new body now. Your *spirit* body."

John nodded. "Uh huh. *Or*...and let me just throw this out there...alternate theory kind of thing...maybe this is all a hallucination. I'm in a coma, being kept alive by machines, dreaming of a new and strange life in an impossible place because I'm too far gone to ever come back all the way. The Brits had a show like that, long after you died. Was pretty good."

"Do you really believe that, John?"

John's gaze was drawn upward again, where he saw two more winged things flapping across the roiling red sky, each of them grinning and clutching the leg of a screaming nude woman. The woman dangled upside down, her giant white breasts jiggling as her face twisted in an expression of endless horror.

He looked at Angela again. “No. I don’t believe it.”

The corners of her mouth twitched, trembling on the edge of amusement. “And why is that?”

“Because in a lot of truly fucked up ways, this place feels far more real than the place I left behind.”

Her smile broadened. “Like a place where society’s polite veneer has been stripped away, exposing and reveling in the grandly terrible truth behind the lie?”

“Um. Sure, something like that.”

A big black boat of a car rolled up to the curb and stopped. A rotting severed head was impaled on a large spike on the hood. He wondered if rotting head hood ornaments came standard with limos in hell. A door opened and a man in chauffeur’s livery popped out. The chauffeur called out a greeting to Angela and came quickly around to their side, where he opened one of the rear doors and stood aside for his passengers to enter. Angela touched the man lightly on the arm as she entered the car and said, “Thank you, David.”

John looked at the man again, a thunderstruck expression on his face.

Holy shit.

It was him all right.

He followed Angela into the car, a question freezing on the tip of his tongue as he slid onto the slick leather seat. The streetwalker who’d accosted him upon his arrival in Hell lay hog-tied across the seat opposite them. She turned her head toward them at their arrival, her eyes wet and imploring as she recognized him. The hooker gurgled at him, spittle flying from the corners of her crimson-stained slit-mouth.

John squinted at her as the chauffeur threw the door shut. “What?”

She gurgled at him again.

It was then that he noticed the pink flap of bloody flesh impaled on one of her stiletto heels.

Her fucking tongue.

John grimaced. "Whoa."

Angela giggled. "You like? She did threaten you, after all."

John looked at her. "Yeah. She did." He frowned. "Is this the surprise you were talking about?"

"No, John. She's merely an appetizer. And I'll not spoil the surprise. You'll just have to wait until we've arrived at your new home."

"Which is where again?"

She beamed at him. "With me, John! In the court of Grand Duke Dracul. You'll be my manservant and trusted aide." Yet another of those girlish giggles that made her sound like a demented teenybopper. "As well as my indefatigable fuck toy."

John gritted his teeth. He wasn't sure how he felt about a life in shackles. It'd been a long, long time since he'd been subservient to anyone, with the glaring exception of the miserable week as Linda's whipped puppy. But he clearly wasn't in a position to argue or rebel. Besides, the life she described sounded as if it would be a dream come true for most residents of the Mephistopolis. He supposed many here would resent his easy ascension to so coveted a position. Which posed another matter of some personal significance. Though he had worked hard to redeem himself through the bulk of his adult life, there was no doubt the likes of John Marlowe deserved to spend eternity in Hell. But he would apparently spend that eternity living in luxury and circulating amongst Hell's power elite. He was no expert on matters spiritual, but he was pretty sure this was not the sort of fate envisioned by the fire and brimstone preachers back on earth for especially egregious sinners. Surely one so vile as The Little Rock Madman should boil forever in a lake of fire.

Angela slid open a cabinet to reveal a fully stocked bar. "Drink, John?"

"If you've got something like bourbon in there, I'll have a double." He eyed the gleaming bottles and reconsidered. "No, make that a triple. And while you're at it, could you please tell me how in the name of blue fucking hell David Hasselhoff could be your chauffeur. The man's not dead yet."

Angela filled two glasses with amber liquid from a smoky black bottle and passed one to John. "Cheers."

They clinked glasses.

"Cheers."

John shivered. The booze had a bite, but was also smooth going down, like liquid nirvana.

Angela closed the bar and settled back into the seat. "Oh, David's been dead since the 80's, John. Before me, even. That thing on earth is a magickal construct, a thing fashioned by skilled Bio-Wizards in Lucifer's most secret laboratories. It bides its time. A moment will come. All the world will be watching. And then..."

John let the implied question hang. Whatever diabolical design Hell had in mind for the Hoff's ringer on earth was something he could live without knowing. Things were weird enough already. Something else had occurred to him while watching Angela shift around in the seat and noted the exquisitely supple way the fabric of the dress adhered to her flesh. Ripples and eddies of white radiance swirled across the dress whenever light hit it in just the right way.

"Your dress. It looks..."

She sipped more of the smoky booze and scooted closer to him, placed a hand on his knee. "You like? It's a one of a kind design. Skin, of course. Human skin. Specially treated and enchanted. An anniversary gift from the Grand Duke."

"Okay."

They finished their drinks and had one more. By then the limo had reached its destination. The door to John's right opened. He stepped past the Hoff and gaped at the huge mansion. It stood like a hulking black beast against the scarlet sky, and it looked like the kind of place Donald Trump would want to call home after his own inevitable arrival in Hell.

John looked at Angela. "Is this..." He gulped. "It couldn't be..."

She took him by the arm again. "It's your new home, darling."

John tried to say something else, but only a wheeze emerged.

Angela laughed. "Come. I'll give you the tour."

The tour was a blur of endless hallways and rooms. Dracul's mansion consisted of seemingly a thousand different wings. The place was awash in decadence. He saw things having frenzied sex with other things. Some of it may even have been consensual. They passed through a kitchen, where a bloated human body was roasting slowly over an open pit. At one point he peered through the open doorway of a bedroom and saw a bound man having his nuts chewed off by a woman in a Nun's habit. After a time that felt like two, maybe three years, they arrived at a spacious set of living quarters, impeccably appointed adjoining rooms. One of the rooms was technically John's, but Angela insisted this was a formality. He would spend nearly all his time with her. When she wasn't attending to the Grand Duke's needs and passions, anyway.

John sat on the edge of a plush bed the size of a houseboat and watched the Hoff dump the still-bound hooker on the floor. Angela dismissed the dead B-lister and the man quietly departed, closing the door behind him.

Angela grinned. "Alone at last." Her gaze flicked briefly to the hooker. "Except for our toy here. Oh..." She put a finger to her red lips. "I almost forgot. Your surprise."

She took him by the hand and pulled him to his feet, then into the other bedroom and on through to a small anteroom.

John gasped.

He didn't say anything for a long time, but Angela was beaming at him again.

Then he began to smile, too.

He walked toward her, bent at the waist to look into her eyes. "Hello, Linda. I can't tell you how happy I am to see you again."

Angela came forward, wound a length of Linda's sweat-stained hair in her hand, and lifted her head up. "John, did Linda ever tell you about the thing she did as a teenager? The thing that Damned her?"

"Probably not."

"She and some friends came across a young black child in their neighborhood. He was lost, wasn't supposed to be there. They took him to an empty house and did nasty things to him, things she confessed to me last night after some hours on the rack. She laughed at his cries when she put a cigarette out in his eye."

John arched an eyebrow. "Huh. No. That's news to me."

Linda tried to tell him something, but he couldn't make it out. Her mouth had been sewn shut. She was locked in a pillory. Nude. Her pendulous breasts and sleek, lithe body shiny with fear-sweat. He unzipped his pants and stepped behind her, did the thing she'd told him he would never do with her again. And while he did it, he noted with pleasure the vast array of torture implements hanging from hooks on the walls. When he was done, he tried out a few of them on her.

But he didn't let himself go too far. Not this time. Not yet.

He had plenty of time to creatively hurt her.

Eternity, in fact.

When he was done playing, he let Angela guide him back to the main room. There he swept Angela into his arms and kissed her with a romantic abandon he hadn't felt since the early days of his courtship of Linda.

She eased out of the embrace after a time and said, "You'll be happy here."

John experienced one last pang of something like conscience, a final dying echo of remorse. Then he thought of Linda in the pillory. Licked his lips and savored the sweet taste of Angela's lips. Looked at the bound hooker and thought of some things that might be fun.

He looked into Angela's sparkling eyes again. "Had a beer at that place. Something called Gein's Mean Imperial Stout."

"You can have it perpetually on tap in your room, if you like."

"That singer. Bon Scott. Could he come over some time, maybe entertain us?"

"He'll have a standing invitation."

John's smile was bemused. "I've been thinking I deserve to be here. You know what I mean."

She angled her body against his, slid against his crotch. "Yes. And you do deserve to be here. Right here. With me. With anything you want as yours for the asking."

He pulled her close, kissed her again, breathing the words into her mouth. "I think you're right. I really do."

They kissed some more.

Made love.

Did some interesting things to the hooker.

Did other, even more interesting things to Linda.

And at some point in the festivities, John came to a conclusion. He was right where some secret part of his heart had always known was his destiny.

His true home, the one that had waited for him with such patience.

And possibly he was even falling in love.

Hell, things couldn't be better.

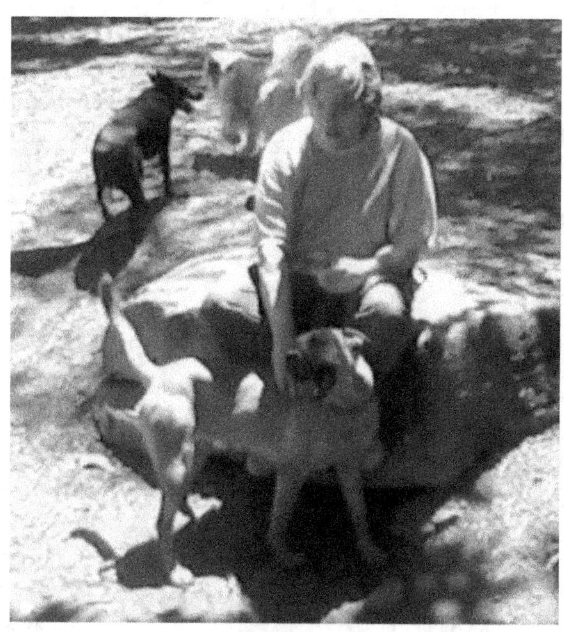

About the Author

Bryan Smith is the author of numerous mass market horror novels, including the popular releases *Depraved*, *The Killing Kind*, and *The Dark Ones*. His full mass market backlist will be reissued by Deadite Press throughout 2011 and 2012. His first title with Deadite Press was the acclaimed novella *Rock And Roll Reform School Zombies*. Another novella, a vampire tale entitled *Bloodrush*, is scheduled for release from Delirium Books in July of 2011. Bryan lives in the middle of Tennessee with a vast array of pets. Visit his home on the web at www.bryansmith.info.

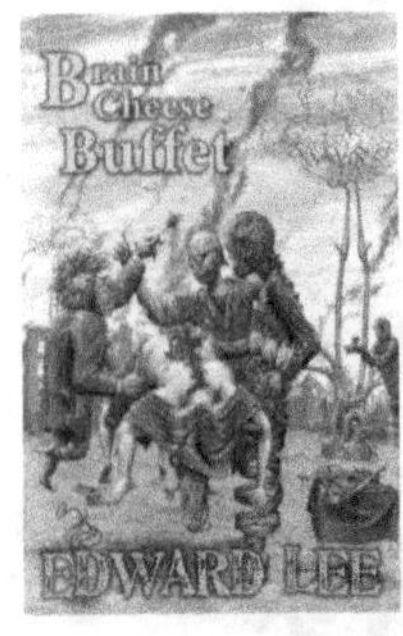

"Brain Cheese Buffet" Edward Lee - collecting nine of Lee's most sought after tales of violence and body fluids. Featuring the Stoker nominated "Mr. Torso," the legendary gross-out piece "The Dritiphilist," the notorious "The McCrath Model SS40-C, Series S," and six more stories to test your gag reflex.

"*Edward Lee's writing is fast and mean as a chain saw revved to full-tilt boogie.*"

- Jack Ketchum

"Bullet Through Your Face" Edward Lee - No writer is more extreme, perverted, or gross than Edward Lee. His world is one of psychopathic redneck rapists, sex addicted demons, and semen stealing aliens. Brace yourself, the king of splatterspunk is guaranteed to shock, offend, and make you laugh until you vomit.

"*Lee pulls no punches.*"

- Fangoria

"Zombies and Shit" Carlton Mellick III - *Battle Royale* meets *Return of the Living Dead* in this post-apocalyptic action adventure. Twenty people wake to find themselves in a boarded-up building in the middle of the zombie wasteland. They soon realize they have been chosen as contestants on a popular reality show called Zombie Survival. Each contestant is given a backpack of supplies and a unique weapon. Their goal: be the first to make it through the zombie-plagued city to the pick-up zone alive. A campy, trashy, punk rock gore fest.

"Slaughterhouse High" Robert Devereaux - It's prom night in the Demented States of America. A place where schools are built with secret passageways, rebellious teens get zippers installed in their mouths and genitals, and once a year one couple is slaughtered and the bits of their bodies are kept as souvenirs. But something's gone terribly wrong when the secret killer starts claiming a far higher body count than usual . . .

"*A major talent!*" - Poppy Z. Brite

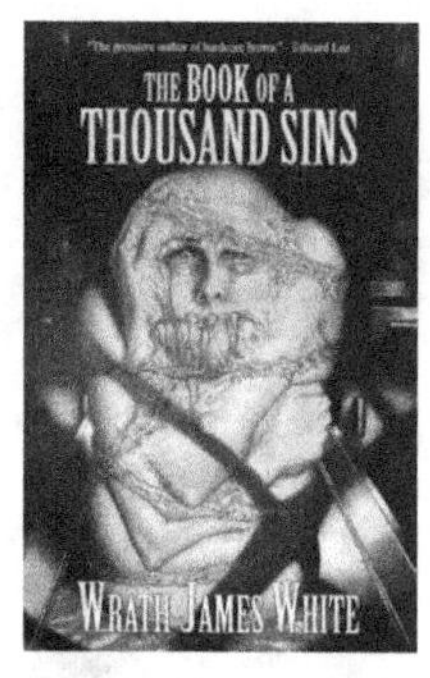

"The Book of a Thousand Sins" Wrath James White - Welcome to a world of Zombie nymphomaniacs, psychopathic deities, voodoo surgery, and murderous priests. Where mutilation sex clubs are in vogue and torture machines are sex toys. No one makes it out alive – not even God himself.

"If Wrath James White doesn't make you cringe, you must be riding in the wrong end of a hearse."

-Jack Ketchum

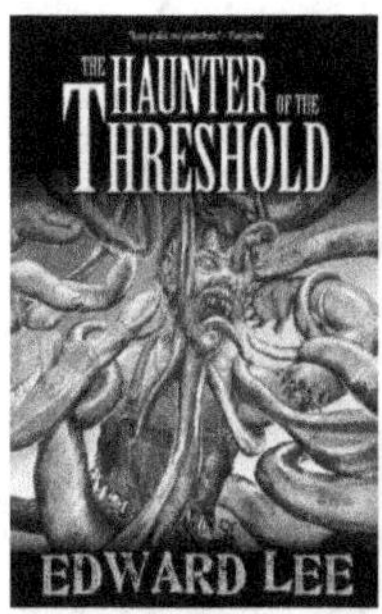

"The Haunter of the Threshold" Edward Lee - There is something very wrong with this backwater town. Suicide notes, magic gems, and haunted cabins await her. Plus the woods are filled with monsters, both human and otherworldly. And then there are the horrible tentacles . . . Soon Hazel is thrown into a battle for her life that will test her sanity and sex drive. The sequel to H.P. Lovecraft's The Haunter of the Dark is Edward Lee's most pornographic novel to date!

"Apeshit" Carlton Mellick III - Friday the 13th meets Visitor Q. Six hipster teens go to a cabin in the woods inhabited by a deformed killer. An incredibly fucked-up parody of B-horror movies with a bizarro slant

"*The new gold standard in unstoppable fetus-fucking kill-freakomania . . . Genuine all-meat hardcore horror meets unadulterated Bizarro brainwarp strangeness. The results are beyond jaw-dropping, and fill me with pure, unforgivable joy.*" - John Skipp

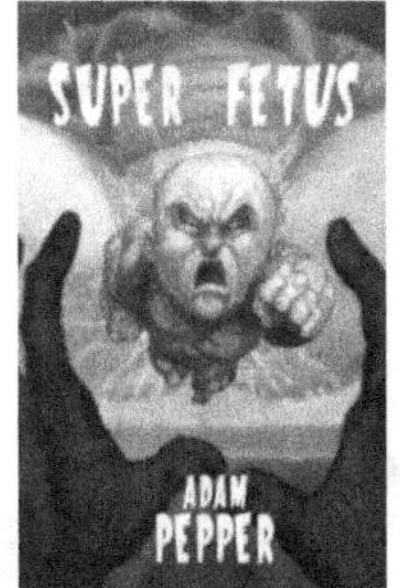

"Super Fetus" Adam Pepper - Try to abort this fetus and he'll kick your ass!

"*The story of a self-aware fetus whose morally bankrupt mother is desperately trying to abort him. This darkly humorous novella will surely appall and upset a sizable percentage of people who read it . . . In-your-face, allegorical social commentary.*"

- BarnesandNoble.com

THE VERY BEST IN CULT HORROR

deadite press

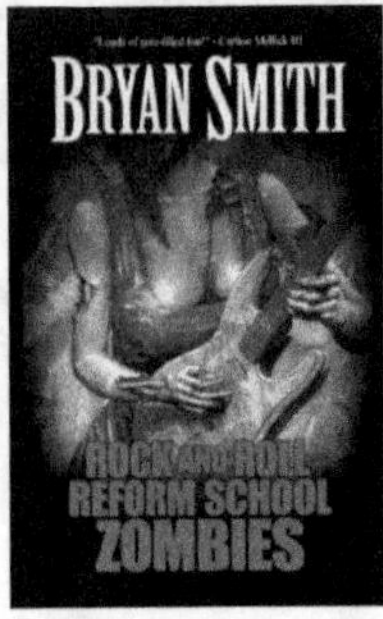

"Rock and Roll Reform School Zombies" Bryan Smith - Sex, Death, and Heavy Metal! The Southern Illinois Music Reeducation Center specializes in "de-metaling" – a treatment to cure teens of their metal loving, devil worshiping ways. A program that subjects its prisoners to sexual abuse, torture, and brain-washing. But tonight things get much worse. Tonight the flesh-eating zombies come . . . *Rock and Roll Reform School Zombies* is Bryan Smith's tribute to "Return of the Living Dead" and "The Decline of Western Civilization Part 2: the Metal Years."

"Necro Sex Machine" Andre Duza - America post apocalypse...a toxic wasteland populated by bloodthirsty scavengers, mutated animals, and roving bands of organized militias wing for control of civilized society's leftovers. Housed in small settlements that pepper the wasteland, the survivors of the third world war struggle to rebuild amidst the scourge of sickness and disease and the constant threat of attack from the horrors that roam beyond their borders. But something much worse has risen from the toxic fog.

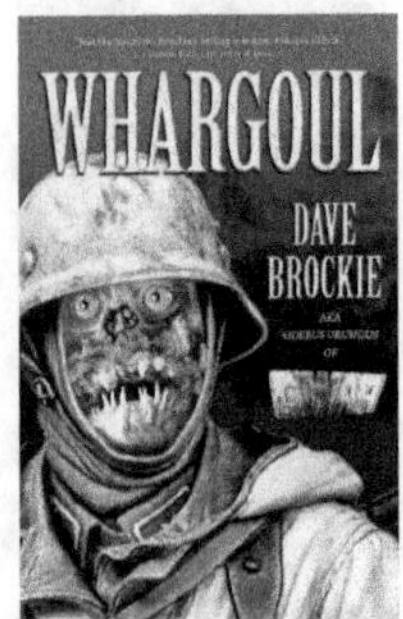

"Whargoul" Dave Brockie - It is a beast born in bullets and shrapnel, feeding off of pain, misery, and hard drugs. Cursed to wander the Earth without the hope of death, it is reborn again and again to spread the gospel of hate, abuse, and genocide. But what if it's not the only monster out there? What if there's something worse? From Dave Brockie, the twisted genius behind GWAR, comes a novel about the darkest days of the twentieth century.

"The Vegan Revolution . . . with Zombies" David Agranoff - Thanks to a new miracle drug the cute little pig no longer feels a thing as she is led to the slaughter. The only problem? Once the drug enters the food supply anyone who eats it is infected. From fast food burgers to free-range organic eggs, eating animal products turns people into shambling brain-dead zombies – not even vegetarians are safe!

"*A perfect blend of horror, humor and animal activism.*"

- Gina Ranalli

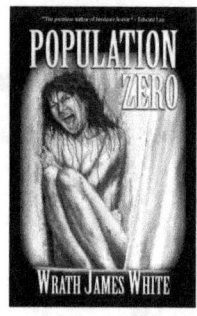

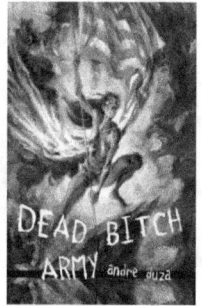

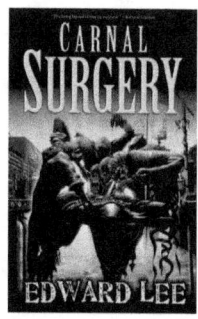

www.ingramcontent.com/pod-product-compliance
Lightning Source LLC
Chambersburg PA
CBHW051657260626
47170CB00004B/1554

* 9 7 8 1 9 3 6 3 8 3 6 8 9 *